Other Avon books by
Roger Zelazny

Roger Zelazny

Sign of the Unicorn

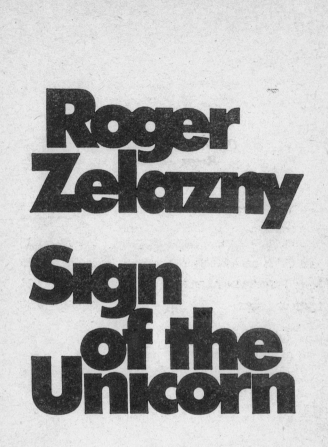

AVON
PUBLISHERS OF BARD, CAMELOT AND DISCUS BOOKS

AVON BOOKS
A division of
The Hearst Corporation
959 Eighth Avenue
New York, New York 10019

Copyright © 1975 by Roger Zelazny
Published by arrangement with Doubleday & Company, Inc.
Library of Congress Catalog Card Number: 74-12722
ISBN: 0-380-00831-9

First Avon Printing, November, 1976
Third Printing

AVON TRADEMARK REG. U.S. PAT. OFF. AND IN
OTHER COUNTRIES, MARCA REGISTRADA,
HECHO EN U S.A.

Printed in the U.S.A.

For Jadawin and his Demiurge,
not to forget Kickaha.

1

I ignored the questions in the eyes of the groom as I lowered the grisly parcel and turned the horse in for care and maintenance. My cloak could not really conceal the nature of its contents as I slung the guts over my shoulder and stamped off toward the rear entrance to the palace. Hell would soon be demanding its paycheck.

I skirted the exercise area and made my way to the trail that led toward the southern end of the palace gardens. Fewer eyes along that route. I would still be spotted, but it would be a lot less awkward than going in the front way, where things are always busy. Damn.

And again, damn. Of troubles I considered myself amply possessed. But those who have do seem to get. Some spiritual form of compound interest, I suppose.

There were a few idlers beside the fountain at the far end of the garden. Also, a couple of guards were passing among the bushes near the trail. The guards saw me coming, held a brief discussion, and looked the other way. Prudent.

Me, back less than a week. Most things, still unresolved. The court of Amber, full of suspicion and unrest. This, now: a death to further jeopardize the brief, unhappy prereign of Corwin I: me.

Time now to do something I should have done right away. But there had been so many things to do, from the very first. It was not as if I had been nodding, as I saw it. I had assigned priorities and acted on them. Now, though . . .

I crossed the garden, out of the shade and into the slanting sunlight. I swung up the wide, curving stair. A guard snapped to attention as I entered the palace. I made for the rear stairway, then up to the second floor. Then the third.

From the right, my brother Random stepped out of his suite and into the hallway.

"Corwin!" he said, studying my face. "What's the matter? I saw you from the balcony and—"

"Inside," I said, gesturing with my eyes. "We are going to have a private conference. Now."

He hesitated, regarding my burden.

"Let's make it two rooms up," he said. "Okay? Vialle's in here."

"All right."

He led the way, opened the door. I entered the small sitting room, sought a likely spot, dropped the body.

Random stared at the bundle.

"What am I supposed to do?" he asked.

"Unwrap the goodies," I said, "and take a look."

He knelt and undid the cloak. He folded it back.

"Dead all right," he observed. "What's the problem?"

"You did not look closely enough," I said. "Peel back an eyelid. Open the mouth and look at the teeth. Feel the spurs on the backs of the hands. Count the joints in the fingers. Then you tell me about the problem."

He began doing these things. As soon as he looked at the hands he stopped and nodded.

"All right," he said. "I remember."

"Remember out loud."

"It was back at Flora's place . . ."

"That was where *I* first saw anyone like this," I said. "They were after you, though. I never did find out why."

"That's right," he said. "I never got a chance to tell you about it. We weren't together all that long. Strange . . . Where did this one come from?"

I hesitated, torn between pushing him from his story

and telling him mine. Mine won out because it was mine and very immediate.

I sighed and sank into a chair.

"We've just lost us another brother," I said. "Caine is dead. I got there a bit too late. That thing—person—did it. I wanted it alive, for obvious reasons. But it put up quite a fight. I didn't have much of a choice."

He whistled softly, seated himself in the chair opposite me.

"I see," he said very softly.

I studied his face. Was that the faintest of smiles waiting in the wings to enter and meet my own? Quite possibly.

"No," I said flatly. "If it were otherwise, I would have arranged for a lot less doubt as to my innocence. I'm telling you what really happened."

"All right," he said. "Where is Caine?"

"Under a layer of sod, near the Grove of the Unicorn."

"That looks suspicious right there," he said. "Or will. To the others."

I nodded.

"I know. I had to hide the body and cover it in the meantime, though. I couldn't just bring him back and start parrying questions. Not when there were important facts waiting for me, in your head."

"Okay," he said. "I don't know how important they are, but they're yours. But don't leave me hanging, huh? How did this thing happen?"

"It was right after lunch," I said. "I had eaten down at the harbor with Gérard. Afterward, Benedict brought me topside through his Trump. Back in my rooms, I found a note which apparently had been slipped in under the door. It requested a private meeting, later in the afternoon, at the Grove of the Unicorn. It was signed 'Caine.' "

"Have you still got the note?"

"Yes." I dug it out of my pocket and passed it to him. "Here."

He studied it and shook his head.

"I don't know," he said. "It *could* be his writing—if he were in a hurry—but I don't think it is."

I shrugged. I took the note back, folded it, put it away.

"Whatever, I tried to reach him with his Trump, to save myself the ride. But he wasn't receiving. I guessed it was to maintain secrecy as to his whereabouts, if it was all that important. So I got a horse and rode on down."

"Did you tell anyone where you were going?"

"Not a soul. I did decide to give the horse a workout, though, so I rode along at a pretty good clip. I didn't see it happen, but I saw him lying there as I came into the wood. His throat had been cut, and there was a disturbance off in the bushes some distance away. I rode the guy down, jumped him, fought with him, had to kill him. We didn't engage in any conversation while this was going on."

"You're sure you got the right guy?"

"As sure as you can be under such circumstances. His trail went back to Caine. He had fresh blood on his garments."

"Might have been his own."

"Look again. No wounds. I broke his neck. Of course I remembered where I had seen his like before, so I brought him right to you. Before you tell me about it, though, there was one more thing—just for a clincher." I withdrew the second note, passed it over. "The creature had this on its person. I presume it had removed it from Caine."

Random read it, nodded, and handed it back.

"From you, to Caine, asking to be met there. Yes, I see. Needless to say . . ."

"Needless to say," I finished. "And it does look a bit like my writing—at first glance, anyway."

"I wonder what would have happened if you had gotten there first?"

"Probably nothing," I said. "Alive and looking bad

—that seems how they wanted me. The trick was to get us there in the proper order, and I didn't hurry quite enough to miss what was bound to follow."

He nodded.

"Granting the tight scheduling," he said, "it had to be someone on the scene, here in the palace. Any ideas?"

I chuckled and reached for a cigarette. I lit it and chuckled again.

"I'm just back. You have been here all along," I said. "Which one hates me the most these days?"

"That is an embarrassing question, Corwin," he stated. "Everyone's down on you for something. Ordinarily, I would nominate Julian. Only it doesn't seem to hold up here."

"Why not?"

"He and Caine got along very well. For years now. They had been looking out for each other, hanging around together. Pretty thick. Julian is cold and petty and just as nasty as you remember. But if he liked anybody, he liked Caine. I don't think he'd do it to him, not even to get at you. After all, he probably could have found plenty of other ways if that was all he wanted."

I sighed.

"Who's next?"

"I don't know. I just don't know."

"Okay. How do you read the reactions to this?"

"You're screwed, Corwin. Everyone is going to think you did it, no matter what you say."

I nodded at the corpse. Random shook his head.

"That could easily be some poor clod you dug up out of Shadow to take the blame."

"I know," I said. "Funny, coming back to Amber as I did, I arrived at an ideal time for positioning myself advantageously."

"A perfect time," Random agreed. "You didn't even have to kill Eric to get what you wanted. That was a stroke of luck."

"Yes. Still, it is no secret that that is what I came to

do, and it is only a matter of time before my troops—foreign, specially armed, and quartered here—are going to start provoking some very bad feelings. Only the presence of an external threat has saved me from that so far. And then there are the things I am suspected of having done before my return—like murdering Benedict's retainers. Now this . . ."

"Yes," Random said, "I saw it coming as soon as you told me. When you and Bleys attacked years ago, Gérard deployed part of the fleet so that it was out of your way. Caine, on the other hand, engaged you with his vessels and scuttled you. Now that he is gone, I imagine you will put Gérard in command of the entire fleet."

"Who else? He is the only man for the job."

"Nevertheless . . ."

"Nevertheless. Admitted. If I were going to kill any one person to strengthen my position, Caine would be the logical choice. That's the real, damning truth."

"How do you propose handling this?"

"Tell everyone what happened and try to discover who was behind it. Have you any better suggestions?"

"I've been trying to think how I could alibi you. But it does not look promising."

I shook my head.

"You are too close to me. No matter how good we made it sound, it would probably have the opposite effect."

"Have you considered admitting to it?"

"Yes. But self-defense is out. With a cut throat, it had to be a matter of surprise. And I have no stomach for starting off with the alternative: hoke up some evidence that he was up to something rotten and say I did it for the good of Amber. I flatly refuse to take on fake guilt under those terms. I'd wind up with a bad odor that way, too."

"But with a real tough reputation."

"It's the wrong kind of tough for the sort of show I want to run. No, that's out."

"That covers everything, then—just about."

"What do you mean 'just about'?"

He studied his left thumbnail through slitted eyes.

"Well, it occurs to me that if there is anyone else you are anxious to get out of the picture, now is the time to consider that a frame can often be shifted."

I thought about it and finished my cigarette.

"Not bad," I said, "but I can't spare any more brothers at the moment. Not even Julian. Anyhow, he's the least frameable."

"It need not be family," he said. "Plenty of noble Amberites around with possible motives. Take Sir Reginald—"

"Forget it, Random The reframing is out, too."

"Okay. I've exhausted my little gray cells, then."

"Not the ones in charge of memory, I hope."

"All right."

He sighed. He stretched. He got to his feet, stepped over the room's other occupant, and made his way to the window. Drawing back the drapes, he stared out for a time.

"All right," he repeated. "There's a lot to tell. . . ."

Then he remembered out loud.

2

While sex heads a great number of lists, we all have other things we like to do in between. With me, Corwin, it's drumming, being up in the air, and gambling —in no special order. Well, maybe soaring has a little edge—in gliders, balloons, and certain variations—but mood has a lot to do with that too, you know. I mean, ask me another time and I might say one of the others. Depends on what you want most at the moment.

Anyway, I was here in Amber some years ago. Not doing much of anything. Just visiting and being a nuisance. Dad was still around, and when I noticed that he was getting into one of his grumpy moods, I decided it was time to take a walk. A long one. I had often noticed that his fondness for me tended to increase as an inverse function of my proximity. He gave me a fancy riding crop for a going-away present—to hasten the process of affection, I suppose. Still, it was a very nice crop—silver-chased, beautifully tooled—and I made good use of it. I had decided to go looking for an assemblage of all my simple pleasures in one small nook of Shadow.

It was a long ride—I will not bore you with the details—and it was pretty far from Amber, as such things go. This time, I was not looking for a place where I would be especially important. That can get either boring or difficult fairly quickly, depending on how responsible you want to be. I wanted to be an irresponsible nonentity and just enjoy myself.

Texorami was a wide open port city, with sultry days

and long nights, lots of good music, gambling around the clock, duels every morning and in-between mayhem for those who couldn't wait. And the air currents were fabulous. I had a little red sail plane I used to go sky surfing in, every couple of days. It was the good life. I played drums till all hours in a basement spot up the river where the walls sweated almost as much as the customers and the smoke used to wash around the lights like streams of milk. When I was done playing I'd go find some action, women, or cards, usually. And that was it for the rest of the night. Damn Eric, anyway! That reminds me again . . . He once accused me of cheating at cards, did you know that? And that's about the only thing I wouldn't cheat at. I take my card playing seriously. I'm good and I'm also lucky. Eric was neither. The trouble with him was that he was good at so many things he wouldn't admit even to himself that there were some things other people could do better. If you kept beating him at anything you had to be cheating. He started a nasty argument over it one night—could have gotten serious—but Gérard and Caine broke it up. Give Caine that. He took my part that time. Poor guy . . . Hell of a way to go, you know? His throat . . . Well, anyhow, there I was in Texorami, making music and women, winning at cards and jockeying around the sky. Palm trees and night-blooming wallflowers. Lots of good port smells—spices, coffee, tar, salt—you know. Gentlefolk, merchants, and peons—the same straights as in most other places. Sailors and assorted travelers passing in and out. Guys like me living around the edges of things. I spent a little over two years in Texorami, happy. Really. Not much contact with the others. Sort of postcardlike hellos via the Trumps every now and then, and that was about it. Amber was pretty much off my mind. All this changed one night when I was sitting there with a full house and the guy across from me was trying to make up his mind whether or not I was bluffing.

The Jack of Diamonds began talking to me.

Yes, that is how it started. I was in a weird frame of mind anyway. I had just finished a couple very hot sets and was still kind of high. Also, I was physically strung out from a long day's gliding and not much sleep the night before. I decided later that it must be our mental quirk associated with the Trumps that made me see it that way when someone was trying to reach me and I had cards in my hand—any cards. Ordinarily, of course, we get the message empty-handed, unless we are doing the calling. It could have been that my subconscious—which was kind of footloose at the time—just seized on the available props out of habit. Later, though, I had cause to wonder. Really, I just don't know.

The Jack said, "Random." Then its face blurred and it said, "Help me." I began getting a feel of the personality by then, but it was weak. The whole thing was very weak. Then the face rearranged itself and I saw that I was right. It was Brand. He looked like hell, and he seemed to be chained or tied to something. "Help me," he said again.

"I'm here," I said. "What's the matter?"

". . . prisoner," he said, and something else that I couldn't make out.

"Where?" I asked.

He shook his head at that.

"Can't bring you through," he said. "No Trumps, and I am too weak. You will have to come the long way around. . . ."

I did not ask him how he was managing it without my Trump. Finding out where he was seemed of first importance. I asked him how I could locate him.

"Look very closely," he said. "Remember every feature. I may only be able to show you once. Come armed, too. . . ."

Then I saw the landscape—over his shoulder, out a window, over a battlement, I can't be sure. It was far from Amber, somewhere where the shadows go mad. Farther than I like to go. Stark, with shifting colors. Fiery. Day without a sun in the sky. Rocks that glided

like sailboats across the land. Brand there in some sort
of tower—a small point of stability in that flowing scene.
I remembered it, all right. And I remembered the
presence coiled about the base of that tower. Brilliant.
Prismatic. Some sort of watch-thing, it seemed—too
bright for me to make out its outline, to guess its proper
size. Then it all just went away. Instant off. And there
I was, staring at the Jack of Diamonds again, with the
guy across from me not knowing whether to be mad at
my long distraction or concerned that I might be having
some sort of sick spell.

I closed up shop with that hand and went home. I
lay stretched out on my bed, smoking and thinking.
Brand had still been in Amber when I had departed.
Later, though, when I had asked after him, no one had
any idea as to his whereabouts. He had been having
one of his melancholy spells, had snapped out of it one
day and ridden off. And that was that. No messages
either—either way. He wasn't answering, he wasn't
talking.

I tried to figure every angle. He was smart, damn
smart. Possibly the best mind in the family. He was in
trouble and he had called me. Eric and Gérard were
more the heroic types and would probably have wel-
comed the adventure. Caine would have gone out of
curiosity, I think. Julian, to look better than the rest of
us and to score points with Dad. Or, easiest of all,
Brand could have called Dad himself. Dad would have
done something about it. But he had called me. Why?

It occurred to me then that maybe one or more of
the others had been responsible for his circumstances.
If, say, Dad was beginning to favor him . . . Well. You
know. Eliminate the positive. And if he did call Dad,
he would look like a weakling.

So I suppressed my impulse to yell for reinforce-
ments. He had called me, and it was quite possible that
I would be cutting his throat by letting anyone back in
Amber in on the fact that he had gotten the message
out. Okay. What was in it for me?

If it involved the succession and he had truly become fair-haired, I figured that I could do a lot worse than give him this to remember me by. And if it did not . . . There were all sorts of other possibilities. Perhaps he had stumbled onto something going on back home, something it would be useful to know about. I was even curious as to the means he had employed for bypassing the Trumps. So it was curiosity, I'd say, that made me decide to go it alone and try to rescue him.

I dusted off my own Trumps and tried reaching him again. As you might expect, there was no response. I got a good night's sleep then and tried one more time in the morning. Again, nothing. Okay, no sense waiting any longer.

I cleaned up my blade, ate a big meal, and got into some rugged clothes. I also picked up a pair of dark, polaroid goggles. Didn't know how they would work there, but that warden-thing had been awfully bright— and it never hurts to try anything extra you can think of. For that matter, I also took a gun. I had a feeling it would be worthless, and I was right. But, like I said, you never know till you try.

The only person I said good-bye to was another drummer, because I stopped to give him my set before I left. I knew he'd take good care of them.

Then I went on down to the hangar, got the sail plane ready, went aloft, and caught a proper current. It seemed a neat way to do it.

I don't know whether you've ever glided through Shadow, but— No? Well, I headed out over the sea till the land was only a dim line to the north. Then I had the waters go cobalt beneath me, rear up and shake sparkly beards. The wind shifted. I turned. I raced the waves shoreward beneath a darkening sky. Texorami was gone when I returned to the rivermouth, replaced by miles of swamp. I rode the currents inward, crossing and recrossing the river at new twists and kinks it had acquired. Gone were the piers, the trails, the traffic. The trees were high.

Clouds massed in the west, pink and pearl and yellow. The sun phased from orange through red to yellow. You shake your head? The sun was the price of the cities, you see. In a hurry, I depopulate—or, rather, go the elemental route. At that altitude artifacts would have been distracting. Shading and texture becomes everything for me. That's what I meant about gliding it being a bit different.

So, I bore to the west till the woods gave way to surface green, which quickly faded, dispersed, broke to brown, tan, yellow. Light and crumbly then, splotched. The price of that was a storm. I rode it out as much as I could, till the lightnings forked nearby and I feared that the gusts were getting to be too much for the little glider. I toned it down fast then, but got more green below as a result. Still, I pulled it out of the storm with a yellow sun firm and bright at my back. After a time, I got it to go desert beneath me again, stark and rolling.

Then the sun shrank and strands of cloud whipped past its face, erasing it bit by bit. That was the shortcut that took me farther from Amber than I had been in a long while.

No sun then, but the light remained, just as bright but eerie now, directionless. It tricked my eyes, it screwed up perspective. I dropped lower, limiting my range of vision. Soon large rocks came into view, and I fought for the shapes I remembered. Gradually, these occurred.

The buckling, flowing effect was easier to achieve under these conditions, but its production was physically disconcerting. It made it even more difficult to judge my effectiveness in guiding the glider. I got lower than I thought I was and almost collided with one of the rocks. Finally, though, the smokes rose and flames danced about as I remembered them—conforming to no particular pattern, just emerging here and there from crevasses, holes, cave mouths. Colors began to misbehave as I recalled from my brief view. Then came the

actual motion of the rocks—drifting, sailing, like rud-
derless boats in a place where they wring out rainbows.

By then, the air currents had gone crazy. One updraft
after another, like fountains, I fought them as best I
could, but knew I could not hold things together much
longer at that altitude. I rose a considerable distance,
forgetting everything for a time while trying to stabilize
the craft. When I looked down again, it was like view-
ing a free-form regatta of black icebergs. The rocks were
racing around, clashing together, backing off, colliding
again, spinning, arcing across the open spaces, passing
among one another. Then I was slammed about, forced
down, forced up—and I saw a strut give way. I gave the
shadows their final nudge, then looked again. The tower
had appeared in the distance, something brighter than
ice or aluminum stationed at its base.

That final push had done it. I realized that just as I
felt the winds start a particularly nasty piece of business. Then several cables snapped and I was on my way
down—like riding a waterfall. I got the nose up,
brought it in low and wild, saw where we were headed,
and jumped at the last moment. The poor glider was
pulverized by one of those peripatetic monoliths. I felt
worse about that than I did about the scrapes, rips, and
lumps I collected.

Then I had to move quickly, because a hill was racing
toward me. We both veered, fortunately in different
directions. I hadn't the faintest notion as to their motive
force, and at first I could see no pattern to their movements. The ground varied from warm to extremely hot
underfoot, and along with the smoke and occasional
jets of flame, nasty-smelling gases were escaping from
numerous openings in the ground. I hurried toward the
tower, following a necessarily irregular course.

It took a long while to cover the distance. Just how
long, I was uncertain, as I had no way of keeping track
of the time. By then, though, I was beginning to notice
some interesting regularities. First, the larger stones
moved at a greater velocity than the smaller ones.

Second, they seemed to be orbiting one another—cycles within cycles within cycles, larger about smaller, none of them ever still. Perhaps the prime mover was a dust mote or a single molecule—somewhere. I had neither time nor desire to indulge in any attempt to determine the center of the affair. Keeping this in mind, I did manage to observe as I went, though, enough so that I was able to anticipate a number of their collisions well in advance.

So Childe Random to the dark tower came, yeah, gun in one hand, blade in the other. The goggles hung about my neck. With all the smoke and confused lighting, I wasn't about to don them until it became absolutely necessary.

Now, whatever the reason, the rocks avoided the tower. While it seemed to stand on a hill, I realized as I approached that it would be more correct to say that the rocks had scooped out an enormous basin just short of it. I could not tell from my side, however, whether the effect was that of an island or a peninsula.

I dashed through the smoke and rubble, avoiding the jets of flame that leaped from the cracks and holes. Finally I scrambled up the slope, removing myself from the courseway. Then for several moments I clung at a spot just below any line of sight from the tower. I checked my weapons, controlled my breathing, and put on the goggles. Everything set, I went over the top and came up into a crouch.

Yes, the shades worked. And yes, the beast was waiting.

It was a fright all right, because in some ways it was kind of beautiful. It had a snake body as big around as a barrel, with a head sort of like a massive claw hammer, but kind of tapered to the snout end. Eyes of a very pale green. And it was clear as glass, with very faint, fine lines seeming to indicate scales. Whatever flowed in its veins was reasonably clear, also. You could look right into it and see its organs—opaque or cloudy as the case might be. You could almost be distracted by watching the thing function. And it had a dense mane, like bristles of glass, about the head and collaring its gullet. Its movement when it saw me, raised that head and slithered forward, was like flowing water—living water, it seemed, a bedless river without banks. What almost froze me, though, was that I could see into its stomach. There was a partly digested man in it.

I raised the gun, aimed at the nearest eye, and squeezed the trigger.

I already told you it didn't work. So I threw the gun, leaped to my left, and sprang in on its right side, going for its eye with my blade.

You know how hard it can be to kill things built along reptilian lines. It decided immediately to try to blind the thing and hack off its tongue as the first order of business. Then, being more than a little fast on my feet, I might have any number of chances to lay in some good ones about the head until I decapitated it. Then let it tie itself in knots till it stopped. I was hoping, too, that it might be sluggish because it was still digesting someone.

If it was sluggish then, I was glad that I hadn't stopped by earlier. It drew its head out of the path of my blade and snapped down over it while I was still off balance. That snout glanced across my chest, and it did feel as if I had been hit by a massive hammer. It knocked me sprawling.

I kept on rolling to get out of range, coming up short near the edge of the embankment. I recovered my footing there while it unwound itself, dragged a lot of weight in my direction, and then reared up and cocked its head again, about fifteen feet above me.

I know damn well that Gérard would have chosen that moment to attack. The big bastard would have strode forward with that monster blade of his and cut the thing in half. Then it probably would have fallen on him and writhed all over him, and he'd have come away with a few bruises. Maybe a bloody nose. Benedict would not have missed the eye. He would have had one in each pocket by then and be playing football with the head while composing a footnote to Clausewitz. But they are genuine hero types. Me, I just stood there holding the blade point upward, both hands on the hilt, my elbows on my hips, my head as far back out of the way as possible. I would much rather have run and called it a day. Only I knew that if I tried it, that head would drop down and smear me.

Cries from within the tower indicated that I had been spotted, but I was not about to look away to see what was going on. Then I began cursing the thing. I wanted it to strike and get it over with, one way or the other.

When it finally did, I shuffled my feet, twisted my body, and swung the point into line with my target.

My left side was partly numbed by the blow, and I felt as if I had been driven a foot into the ground. Somehow I managed to remain upright. Yes, I had done everything perfectly. The maneuver had gone exactly as I had hoped and planned.

Except for the beast's part. It wasn't cooperating by producing the appropriate death throes.

In fact, it was beginning to rise.

It took my blade with it, too. The hilt protruded from its left eye socket, the point emerged like another bristle amid the mane on the back of its head. I had a feeling that the offensive team had had it.

At that moment, figures began to emerge—slowly, cautiously—from an opening at the base of the tower. They were armed and ugly-looking, and I had a feeling that they were not on my side of the disagreement.

Okay. I know when it is time to fold and hope for a better hand another day.

"Brand!" I shouted. "It's Random! I can't get through! Sorry!"

Then I turned, ran, and leaped back over the edge, down into the place where the rocks did their unsettling things. I wondered whether I had chosen the best time to descend.

Like so many things, the answer was yes and no.

It was not the sort of jump I would make for many reasons other than those which prevailed. I came down alive, but that seemed the most that could be said for it. I was stunned, and for a long while I thought I had broken my ankle.

The thing that got me moving again was a rustling sound from above and the rattle of gravel about me. When I readjusted the goggles and looked up, I saw that the beast had decided to come down and finish the job. It was winding its phantom way down the slope, the area about its head having darkened and opaqued since I had skewered it upstairs.

I sat up. I got to my knees. I tried my ankle, couldn't use it. Nothing around to serve as a crutch, either. Okay. I crawled then. Away. What else was there to do? Gain as much ground as I could and think hard while I was about it.

Salvation was a rock—one of the smaller, slower ones, only about the size of a moving van. When I saw it approaching, it occurred to me that here was transportation if I could make it aboard. Maybe some safety, too. The faster, really massive ones appeared to get the most abuse.

This in mind, I watched the big ones that accompanied my own, estimated their paths and velocities, tried to gauge the movement of the entire system, readied myself for the moment, the effort. I also listened to the approach of the beast, heard the cries of the troops from the edge of the bluff, wondered whether anyone up there was giving odds on me and what they might be if they were.

When the time came, I went. I got past the first big one without any trouble, but had to wait for the next one to go by. I took a chance in crossing the path of the final one. Had to, to make it in time.

I made it to the right spot at the right moment, caught on to the holds I had been eyeing, and was dragged maybe twenty feet before I could pull myself up off the ground. Then I hauled my way to its uncomfortable top, sprawled there, and looked back.

It had been close. Still was, for that matter, as the beast was pacing me, its one good eye following the spinning big ones.

From overhead I heard a disappointed wail. Then the guys started down the slope, shouting what I took to be encouragement to the creature. I commenced massaging my ankle. I tried to relax. The brute crossed over, passing behind the first big rock as it completed another orbit.

How far could I shift through Shadow before it reached me? I wondered. True, there was constant movement, a changing of textures . . .

The thing waited for the second rock, slithered by behind it, paced me again, drew nearer.

Shadow, Shadow, on the wing—

The men were almost to the base of the slope by then. The beast was waiting for its opening—the next time around—past the inner satellite. I knew that it was capable of rearing high enough to snatch me from my perch.

—Come alive and smear that thing!

As I spun and glided I caught hold of the stuff of Shadow, sank into the feel of it, worked with the textures, possible to probable to actual, felt it coming with the finest twist, gave it that necessary fillip at the appropriate moment . . .

It came in from the beast's blind side, of course. A big mother of a rock, careening along like a semi out of control . . .

It would have been more elegant to mash it between two of them. However, I hadn't the time for finesse. I simply ran it over and left it there, thrashing in the granite traffic.

Moments later, however, inexplicably, the mashed and mangled body rose suddenly above the ground and drifted skyward, twisting. It kept going, buffeted by the winds, dwindling, dwindling, gone.

My own rock bore me away, slowly, steadily. The entire pattern was drifting. The guys from the tower then went into a huddle and decided to pursue me. They moved away from the base of the slope, began to make their way across the plain. But this was no real problem, I felt. I would ride my stony mount through Shadow, leaving them worlds away. This was by far the easiest course of action open to me. They would doubtless have been more difficult to take by surprise than the beast. After all, this was their land; they were wary and unmaimed.

I removed the goggles and tested my ankle again. I stood for a moment. It was very sore, but it bore my weight. I reclined once more and turned my thoughts to what had occurred. I had lost my blade and I was now in less than top shape. Rather than go on with the venture under these conditions, I knew that I was doing the safest, wisest thing by getting the hell out. I had gained enough knowledge of the layout and the conditions for my chances to be better next time around. All right . . .

The sky brightened above me, the colors and shadings lost something of their arbitrary, meandering habit. The flames began to subside about me. Good. Clouds started to find their ways across the sky. Excellent. Soon a localized glow began behind a cloudbank. Superb. When it went away, a sun would hang once again in the heavens.

I looked back and was surprised to see that I was still being pursued. However, it could easily be that I had not dealt properly with their analogues for this slice of Shadow. It is never good to assume that you have taken care of everything when you are in a hurry. So . . .

I shifted again. The rock gradually altered its course, shifted its shape, lost its satellites, moved in a straight line toward what was to become the west. Above me, the clouds dispersed and a pale sun shone down. We picked up speed. That should have taken care of everything right there. I had positively come into a different place.

But it had not. When I looked again, they were still coming. True, I had gained some distance on them. But the party trooped right along after me.

Well, all right. Things like that can sometimes happen. There were of course two possibilities. My mind still being more than a little disturbed from all that had just occurred, I had not performed ideally and had drawn them along with me. Or, I had maintained a constant where I should have suppressed a variable—that is, shifted into a place and unconsciously required that the pursuit element be present. Different guys then, but still chasing me.

I rubbed my ankle some more. The sun brightened toward orange. A wind out of the north raised a screen of dust and sand and hung it at my back, removing the gang from my sight. I raced on into the west, where a line of mountains had now grown up. Time was in a distortion phase. My ankle felt a little better.

I rested a while. Mine was reasonably comfortable, as rocks go. No sense turning it into a hellride when everything seemed to be proceeding smoothly. I stretched out, hands behind my head, and watched the mountains draw nearer. I thought about Brand and the tower. That was the place all right. Everything was just as it had been in the glimpse he had given me. Except for the guards, of course. I decided that I would cut through the proper piece of Shadow, recruit a cohort of my own, then go back and give them hell. Yes, then everything would be fine. . . .

After a time, I stretched, rolled over onto my stomach, and looked back. Damned if they weren't still following me! They had even gained some.

Naturally, I got angry. To hell with flight! They were asking for it, and it was time they got it.

I rose to my feet. My ankle was only half sore, a little numb. I raised my arms and looked for the shadows I wanted. I found them.

Slowly the rock swung out from its straight course into an arc, turning off to the right. The curve tightened. I swung through a parabola and headed back toward them, my velocity gradually increasing as I went. No time to raise a storm at my back, though I thought that would have been a nice touch if I could have managed it.

As I swept down upon them—there were maybe two dozen—they prudently began to scatter. A number of them didn't make it, though. I swung through another curve and returned as soon as I could.

I was shaken by the sight of several corpses rising into the air, dripping gore, two of them already high above me.

I was almost upon them on that second pass when I realized that a few of them had jumped aboard as I had gone through. The first one over the edge drew his blade and rushed me. I blocked his arm, took the weapon away from him, and threw him back down. I guess it was then that I became aware of those spurs on the backs of their hands. I had been slashed by his.

By that time I was the target of a number of curiously shaped missiles from below, two more guys were coming over the edge, and it looked as if several more might have made it aboard.

Well, even Benedict sometimes retreats. I had at least given the survivors something to remember.

I let go of the shadows, tore a barbed wheel from my side, another from my thigh, hacked off a guy's swordarm and kicked him in the stomach, dropped to my knees to avoid a wild swing from the next one, and caught him across the legs with my riposte. He went over, too.

There were five more on the way up and we were sailing westward once again, leaving perhaps a dozen live ones to regroup on the sand at my back, a sky full of oozing drifters above them.

I had the advantage with the next fellow because

I caught him just partway over the edge. So much for him, and then there were four.

While I had been dealing with him, though, three more had arisen, simultaneously, at three different points.

I rushed the nearest and dispatched him, but the other two made it over and were upon me while I was about it. As I defended myself from their attack, the final one came up and joined them.

They were not all that good, but it was getting crowded and there were a lot of points and sharp edges straying about me. I kept parrying and moving, trying to get them to block one another, get in each other's way. I was partly successful, and when I had the best lineup I thought I was going to get, I rushed them, taking a couple of cuts—I had to lay myself open a bit to do it—but splitting one skull for my pains. He went over the edge and took the second one with him in a tangle of limbs and gear.

Unfortunately, the inconsiderate lout had carried off my blade, snagged in some bony cleft or other he had chosen to interpose when I swung. It was obviously my day for losing blades, and I wondered if my horoscope would have mentioned it if I had thought to look before I'd set out.

Anyhow, I moved quickly to avoid the final guy's swing. In doing so, I slipped on some blood and went skidding toward the front of the rock. If I went down that way, it would plow right over me, leaving a very flat Random there, like an exotic rug, to puzzle and delight future wayfarers.

I clawed for handholds as I slid, and the guy took a couple of quick steps toward me, raising his blade to do unto me as I had his buddy.

I caught hold of his ankle, though, and it did the trick of braking me very nicely—and damned if someone shouldn't choose that moment to try to get hold of me via the Trumps.

"I'm busy!" I shouted. "Call back later!" and my

own motion was arrested as the guy toppled, clattered, and went sliding by.

I tried to reach him before he fell to rugdom, but I was not quite quick enough. I had wanted to save him for questioning. Still, my unegged beer was more than satisfactory. I headed back top and center to observe and muse.

The survivors were still following me, but I had a sufficient lead. I did not at the moment have to worry about another boarding party. Good enough. I was headed toward the mountains once again. The sun I had conjured was beginning to bake me. I was soaked with sweat and blood. My wounds were giving me trouble. I was thirsty. Soon, soon, I decided, it would have to rain. Take care of that before anything else.

So I began the preliminaries to a shift in that direction: clouds massing, building, darkening. . . .

I drifted off somewhere along the line, had a disjointed dream of someone trying to reach me again but not making it. Sweet darkness.

I awakened to the rain, sudden and hard-driving. I could not tell whether the darkness in the sky was from storm, evening, or both. It was cooler, though, and I spread my cloak and just lay there with my mouth open. Periodically I wrung moisture from the cloak. My thirst was eventually slaked and I began feeling clean again. The rock had also become so slick-looking that I was afraid to move about on it. The mountains were much nearer, their peaks limned by frequent lightnings. Things were too dark in the opposite direction for me to tell whether my pursuers were still with me. It would have been pretty rough trekking for them to have kept up, but then it is seldom good policy to rely on assumptions when traveling through strange shadows. I was a bit irritated with myself for going to sleep, but since no harm had come of it I drew my soggy cloak about me and decided to forgive myself. I felt around for some cigarettes I had brought along and found that about half of them had survived. After the eighth try, I juggled shadows enough to get a light. Then I just sat there, smoking and being rained on. It was a good feeling and I didn't move to change anything else, not for hours.

When the storm finally let up and the sky came clear, it was a night full of strange constellations. Beautiful though, the way nights can be on the desert. Much later, I detected a gentle upward sloping and my rock started to slow. Something began happening in terms of whatever physical rules controlled the situation. I mean, the slope itself did not seem so pronounced that it would affect our velocity as radically as it had. I did not want to tamper with Shadow in a direction that would probably take me out of my way. I wanted to get back onto more familiar turf as soon as possible—find my way to a place where my gut anticipations of physical events had more of a chance of being correct.

So I let the rock grind to a halt, climbed down when it did, and continued on up the slope, hiking. As I went, I played the Shadow game we all learned as children. Pass some obstruction—a scrawny tree, a stand of stone—and have the sky be different from one side to the other. Gradually I restored familiar constellations. I knew that I would be climbing down a different mountain from the one I ascended. My wounds still throbbed dully, but my ankle had stopped bothering me except for a little stiffness. I was rested. I knew that I could go for a long while. Everything seemed to be all right again.

It was a long hike, up the gradually steepening way. But I hit a trail eventually, and that made things easier. I trudged steadily upward under the now familiar skies, determined to keep moving and make it across by morning. As I went, my garments altered to fit the shadow—denim trousers and jacket now, my wet cloak a dry serape. I heard an owl nearby, and from a great distance below and behind came what might have been the yipyip-howl of a coyote. These signs of a more familiar place made me feel somewhat secure, exorcised any vestiges of desperation that remained with my flight.

An hour or so later, I yielded to the temptation to play with Shadow just a bit. It was not all that improbable for a stray horse to be wandering in these hills, and of course I found him. After ten or so minutes of becoming friendly, I was mounted bareback and moving toward the top in a more congenial fashion. The wind sowed frost in our path. The moon came and sparked it to life.

To be brief, I rode all night, passing over the crest and commencing my downward passage well before dawn. As I descended, the mountain grew even more vast above me, which of course was the best time for this to occur. Things were green on this side of the range, and divided by neat highways, punctuated by occasional dwellings. Everything therefore was proceeding in accordance with my desire.

Early morning. I was into the foothills and my denim had turned to khaki and a bright shirt. I had a light sport jacket slung before me. At a great height, a jetliner poked holes in the air, moving from horizon to horizon. There were birdsongs about me, and the day was mild, sunny.

It was about then that I heard my name spoken and felt the touch of the Trump once more. I drew up short and responded.

"Yes?"

It was Julian.

"Random, where are you?" he asked.

"Pretty far from Amber," I replied. "Why?"

"Have any of the others been in touch with you?"

"Not recently," I said. "But someone did try to get hold of me yesterday. I was busy though, and couldn't talk."

"That was me," he said. "We have a situation here that you had better know about."

"Where are you?" I asked.

"In Amber. A number of things have happened recently."

"Like what?"

"Dad has been gone for an unusually long time. No one knows where."

"He's done that before."

"But not without leaving instructions and making delegations. He always provided them in the past."

"True," I said. "But how long is 'long'?"

"Well over a year. You weren't aware of this at all?"

"I knew that he was gone. Gérard mentioned it some time back."

"Then add more time to that."

"I get the idea. How have you been operating?"

"That is the problem. We have simply been dealing with affairs as they arise. Gérard and Caine had been running the navy anyway, on Dad's orders. Without him, they have been making all their own decisions. I took charge of the patrols in Arden again. There is no central authority though, to arbitrate, to make policy decisions, to speak for all of Amber."

"So we need a regent. We can cut cards for it, I suppose."

"It is not that simple. We think Dad is dead."

"Dead? Why? How?"

"We have tried to raise him on his Trump. We have been trying every day for over half a year now. Nothing. What do you think?"

I nodded.

"He may be dead," I said. "You'd think he would have come across with something. Still, the possibility of his being in some trouble—say, a prisoner somewhere— is not precluded."

"A cell can't stop the Trumps. Nothing can. He would call for help the minute we made contact."

"I can't argue with that," I said. But I thought of Brand as I said it. "Perhaps he is deliberately resisting contact, though."

"What for?"

"I have no idea, but it is possible. You know how secretive he is about some things."

"No," Julian said, "it doesn't hold up. He would have given some operating instructions, somewhere along the line."

"Well, whatever the reasons, whatever the situation, what do you propose doing now?"

"Someone has to occupy the throne," he said.

I had seen it coming throughout the entire dialogue, of course—the opportunity it had long seemed would never come to pass.

"Who?" I asked.

"Eric seems the best choice," he replied. "Actually, he has been acting in that capacity for months now. It simply becomes a matter of formalizing it."

"Not just as regent?"

"Not just as regent."

"I see . . . Yes, I guess that things have been happening in my absence. What about Benedict as a choice?"

"He seems to be happy where he is, off somewhere in Shadow."

"What does he think of the whole idea?"

"He is not entirely in favor of it. But we do not believe he will offer resistance. It would disrupt things too much."

"I see," I said again. "And Bleys?"

"He and Eric had some rather heated discussions of the issue, but the troops do not take their orders from Bleys. He left Amber about three months ago. He could cause some trouble later. But then, we are forewarned."

"Gérard? Caine?"

"They will go along with Eric. I was wondering about yourself."

"What about the girls?"

He shrugged.

"They tend to take things lying down. No problem."

"I don't suppose Corwin . . ."

"Nothing new. He's dead. We all know it. His monument has been gathering dust and ivy for centuries. If not, then he has intentionally divorced himself from Amber forever. Nothing there. Now I am wondering where you stand."

I chuckled.

"I am hardly in a position to possess forceful opinions," I said.

"We need to know now."

I nodded.

"I have always been able to detect the quarter of the wind," I said. "I do not sail against it."

He smiled and returned my nod.

"Very good," he said.

"When is the coronation? I assume that I am invited."

"Of course, of course. But the date has not yet been set. There are still a few minor matters to be dealt with. As soon as the affair is calendared, one of us will contact you again."

"Thank you, Julian."

"Good-bye for now, Random."

And I sat there being troubled for a long while before I started on downward again. How long had Eric spent engineering it? I wondered. Much of the politicking back in Amber could have been done pretty quickly, but the setting up of the situation in the first place seemed the product of long-term thinking and planning. I was naturally suspicious as to his involvement in Brand's predicament. I also could not help but give some thought to the possibility of his having a hand in Dad's disappearance. That would have taken some doing and have required a really foolproof trap. But the more I thought of it, the less I was willing to put it past him. I even dredged up some old speculations as to his part in your own passing, Corwin. But, offhand, I could not think of a single thing to do about any of it. Go along with it, I figured, if that's where the power was. Stay in his good graces.

Still . . . One should always get more than one angle

on a story. I tried to make up my mind as to who would give me a good one. While I was thinking along these lines, something caught my eye as I glanced back and up, appreciating anew the heights from which I had not quite descended.

There were a number of riders up near the top. They had apparently traversed the same trail I had taken. I could not get an exact nose count, but it seemed suspiciously close to a dozen—a fairly sizable group to be out riding at just that place and time. As I saw that they were proceeding on down the same way that I had come, I had a prickly feeling along the base of my neck. What if . . . ? What if they were the same guys? Because I felt that they were.

Individually, they were no match for me. Even a couple of them together had not made that great a showing. That was not it. The real chiller was that if that's who it was, then we were not alone in our ability to manipulate Shadow in a very sophisticated fashion. It meant that someone else was capable of a stunt that for all my life I had thought to be the sole property of our family. Add to this the fact that they were Brand's wardens, and their designs on the family—at least part of it—did not look all that clement. I perspired suddenly at the notion of enemies who could match our greatest power.

Of course, they were too far off for me to really know just then whether that was truly who it was. But you have to explore every contingency if you want to keep winning the survival game. Could Eric have found or trained or created some special beings to serve him in this particular capacity? Along with you and Eric, Brand had one of the firmest claims on the succession. . . . not to take anything away from your case, damn it! Hell! You know what I mean. I have to talk about it to show you how I was thinking at the time. That's all. So, Brand had had the basis for a pretty good claim if he had been in a position to press it. You being out of the picture, he was Eric's chief rival when it

came to adding a legal touch to things. Putting that together with his plight and the ability of those guys to
traverse Shadow, Eric came to look a lot more sinister
to me. I was more scared by that thought than I was
by the riders themselves, though they did not exactly
fill me with delight. I decided that I had better do several things quickly: talk to someone else in Amber, and
have him take me through the Trump.

Okay. I decided quickly. Gérard seemed the safest
choice. He is reasonably open, neutral. Honest about
most things. And from what Julian had said, Gérard's
role in the whole business seemed kind of passive. That
is, he was not going to resist Eric's move actively. He
would not want to cause a lot of trouble. Didn't mean
he approved. He was probably just being safe and con-
servative old Gérard. That decided, I reached for my
deck of Trumps and almost howled. They were gone.

I searched every pocket in every garment about me.
I had taken them along when I'd left Texorami. I could
have lost them at any point in the previous day's action. I had certainly been battered and thrown about
a lot. And it had been a great day for losing things.
I composed a complicated litany of curses and dug my
heels into the horse's sides. I was going to have to move
fast and think faster now. The first thing would be to
get into a nice, crowded, civilized place where an
assassin of the more primitive sort would be at a dis-
advantage.

As I hurried downhill, heading for one of the roads,
I worked with the stuff of Shadow—quite subtly this
time, using every bit of skill I could muster. There were
just two things I desired at the moment: a final assault
on my possible trackers and a fast path to a place of
sanctuary.

The world shimmered and did a final jig, becoming
the California I had been seeking. A rasping, growling
noise reached my ears, for the final touch I had intended. Looking back, I saw a section of cliff face

come loose, almost in slow motion, and slide directly toward the horsemen. A while later, I had dismounted and was walking in the direction of the road, my garments even fresher and of better quality. I was uncertain as to the time of year, and I wondered what the weather was like in New York.

Before very long, the bus that I had anticipated approached and I flagged it down. I located a window seat, smoked for a while, and watched the countryside. After a time, I dozed.

I did not wake until early afternoon, when we pulled into a terminal. I was ravenous by then, and decided I had better have something to eat before getting a cab to the airport. So I bought three cheeseburgers and a couple of malts with a few of my quondam Texorami greenbacks. Getting served and eating took me maybe twenty minutes. Leaving the snack bar, I saw that there were a number of taxis standing idle at the stand out front. Before I picked one up, though, I decided to make an important stop in the men's room.

At the very damnedest moment you can think of, six stalls flew open behind my back and their occupants rushed me. There was no mistaking the spurs on the backs of their hands, the oversized jaws, the smoldering eyes. Not only had they caught up with me, they were now clad in the same acceptable garb as anyone else in the neighborhood. Gone were any remaining doubts as to their power over Shadow.

Fortunately, one of them was faster than the others. Also, perhaps because of my size, they still might not have been fully aware of my strength. I seized that first one high up on the arm, avoiding those hand bayonets he sported, pulled him over in front of me, picked him up, and threw him at the others. Then I just turned and ran. I broke the door on the way out. I didn't even pause to zip up until I was in a taxi and had the driver burning rubber.

Enough. It was no longer simple sanctuary that I

had in mind. I wanted to get hold of a set of Trumps and tell someone else in the family about those guys. If they were Eric's creatures, the others ought to be made aware of them. If they were not, then Eric ought to be told, too. If they could make their way through Shadow like that, perhaps others could, also. Whatever they represented might one day constitute a threat to Amber herself. Supposing—just supposing—that no one back home was involved? What if Dad and Brand were the victims of a totally unsuspected enemy? Then there was something big and menacing afoot, and I had stepped right into it. That would be an excellent reason for their hounding me this thoroughly. They would want me pretty badly. My mind ran wild. They might even be harrying me toward some sort of a trap. No need for the visible ones to be the only ones about.

I brought my emotions to heel. One by one, you must deal with those things that come to hand, I told myself. That is all. Divorce the feelings from the speculations, or at least provide for separate maintenance. This is sister Flora's shadow. She lives on the other edge of the continent in a place called Westchester. Get to a phone, get hold of information, and call her. Tell her it is urgent and ask for sanctuary. She can't refuse you that, even if she does hate your guts. Then jump a jet and get the hell over there. Speculate on the way if you want, but keep cool now.

So I telephoned from the airport and you answered it, Corwin. That was the variable that broke all the possible equations I had been juggling—you suddenly showing up at that time, that place, that point in events. I grabbed for it when you offered me protection, and not just because I wanted protection. I could probably have taken those six guys out by myself. But that was no longer it. *I thought they were yours.* I figured you had been lying low all along, waiting for the right moment to move in. Now, I thought, you were ready. This explains everything. You had taken our Brand

and you were about to use your Shadow-walking zombies for purposes of going back and catching Eric with his pants down. I wanted to be on your side because I hated Eric and because I knew you were a careful planner and you usually get what you go after. I mentioned the pursuit by guys out of Shadow to see what you would say. The fact that you said nothing didn't really prove anything, though. Either you were being cagey, I figured, or you had no way of knowing where I had been. I also thought of the possibility of walking into a trap of your devising, but I was already in trouble and did not see that I was so important to the balance of power that you would want to dispose of me. Especially if I offered my support, which I was quite willing to do. So I flew on out. And damned if those six didn't board later and follow me. Is he giving me an escort? I wondered. Better not start making more assumptions. I shook them again when we landed, and headed for Flora's place. Then I acted as if none of my guesses had occurred, waiting to see what you would do. When you helped me dispose of the guys, I was really puzzled. Were you genuinely surprised, or was it a put-on, with you sacrificing a few of the troops to keep me ignorant of something? All right, I decided, be ignorant, cooperate, see what he has in mind. I was a perfect setup for that act you pulled to cover the condition of your memory. When I did learn the truth, it was simply too late. We were headed for Rebma and none of this would have meant anything to you. Later, I didn't care to tell Eric anything after his coronation. I was his prisoner then and not exactly kindly disposed toward him. It even occurred to me that my information might be worth something one day—at least, my freedom again—if that threat ever materialized. As for Brand, I doubt anyone would have believed me; and even if someone did, I was the only one who knew how to reach that shadow. Could you see Eric buying that as a reason for releasing me? He would have laughed and told me to come up with a better story. And I never heard from Brand again. None of the others seem to have heard from him either. Odds are he's dead by now—I'd say. And that is the story I never got to tell you. You figure out what it all means.

3

I studied Random, remembering what a great card player he was. By looking at his face, I could no more tell whether he was lying, in whole or in part, than I could learn by scrutinizing the Jack of, say, Diamonds. Nice touch, that part, too. There was enough of that kind of business to his story to give it some feel of verisimilitude.

"To paraphrase Oedipus, Hamlet, Lear, and all those guys," I said, "I wish I had known this some time ago."

"This was the first chance I really had to tell you," he said.

"True," I agreed. "Unfortunately, it not only fails to clarify things, it complicates the puzzle even more. Which is no mean trick. Here we are with a black road running up to the foot of Kolvir. It passes through Shadow, and things have succeeded in traversing it to beset Amber. We do not know the exact nature of the forces behind it, but they are obviously malign and they seem to be growing in strength. I have been feeling guilty about it for some while now, because I see it as being tied in with my curse. Yes, I laid one on us. Curse or no curse, though, everything eventually resolves into some sort of tangibility that can be combatted. Which is exactly what we are going to do. But all week long I have been trying to figure out Dara's part in things. Who is she really? What is she? Why was she so anxious to try the Pattern? How is it that she managed to succeed? And that final threat of hers . . .

43

'Amber will be destroyed,' she said. It seems more than coincidental that this occurred at the same time as the attack over the black road. I do not see it as a separate thing, but as a part of the same cloth. And it all seems to be tied in with the fact that there is a traitor somewhere here in Amber—Caine's death, the notes . . . Someone here is either abetting an external enemy or is behind the whole thing himself. Now you link it all up with Brand's disappearance, by way of this guy." I nudged the corpse with my foot. "It makes it look as if Dad's death or absence is also a part of it. If that is the case, though, it makes for a major conspiracy—with detail after detail having been carefully worked out over a period of years."

Random explored a cupboard in the corner, produced a bottle and a pair of goblets. He filled them and brought me one, then returned to his chair. We drank a silent toast to futility.

"Well," he said, "plotting is the number-one pastime around here, and everyone *has* had plenty of time, you know. We are both too young to remember brothers Osric and Finndo, who died for the good of Amber. But the impression I get from talking with Benedict—"

"Yes," I said, "—that they had done more than wishful thinking about the throne, and it became necessary that they die bravely for Amber. I've heard that, too. Maybe so, maybe not. We'll never know for sure. Still . . . Yes, the point is well taken, though almost unnecessary. I do not doubt that it has been tried before. I do not put it past a number of us. Who, though? We will be operating under a severe handicap until we find out. Any move that we make externally will probably only be directed against a limb of the beast. Come up with an idea."

"Corwin," he said, "to be frank about it, I could make a case for it being anyone here—even myself, prisoner status and all. In fact, something like that would be a great blind for it. I would have taken genuine delight in looking helpless while actually pulling the strings that made all the others dance. Any of us would, though. We all have our motives, our ambitions. And over the years we all have had time and opportunity to lay a lot of groundwork. No, that is the wrong way to go about it, looking for suspects. Everyone here falls into that category. Let us decide instead what it is that would distinguish such an individual, aside from motives, apart from opportunities. I would say, let's look at the methods involved."

"All right. Then you start."

"Some one of us knows more than the rest of us about the workings of Shadow—the ins and the outs, the whys and the hows. He also has allies, obtained from somewhere fairly far afield. This is the combination he has brought to bear upon Amber. Now, we have no way of looking at a person and telling whether he possesses such special knowledge and skills. But let us consider where he could have obtained them. It could be that he simply learned something off in Shadow somewhere, on his own. Or he could have been studying all along, here, while Dworkin was still alive and willing to give lessons."

I stared down into my glass. Dworkin could *still* be living. He had provided my means of escape from the dungeons of Amber—how long ago? I had told no one this, and was not about to. For one thing, Dworkin was quite mad—which was apparently why Dad had had him locked away. For another, he had demonstrated powers I did not understand, which convinced me he could be quite dangerous. Still, he had been kindly disposed toward me after a minimum of flattery and reminiscence. If he were still around, I suspected that with a bit of patience I might be able to handle him. So I had kept the whole business locked away in my mind as a possible secret weapon. I saw no reason for changing that decision at this point.

"Brand did hang around him a lot," I acknowledged, finally seeing what he was getting at. "He was interested in things of that sort."

"Exactly," Random replied. "And he obviously knew more than the rest of us, to be able to send me that message without a Trump."

"You think he made a deal with outsiders, opened the way for them, then discovered that they no longer needed him when they hung him out to dry?"

"Not necessarily. Though I suppose that is possible, too. My thinking runs more like this—and I don't deny my prejudice in his favor: I think he had learned enough about the subject so that he was able to detect it when someone did something peculiar involving the Trumps, the Pattern, or that area of Shadow most adjacent to Amber. Then he slipped up. Perhaps he underestimated the culprit and confronted him directly, rather than going to Dad or Dworkin. What then? The guilty party subdued him and imprisoned him in that tower. Either he thought enough of him not to want to kill him if he did not have to, or he had some later use of him in mind."

"You make that sound plausible, too," I said, and I would have added, "and it fits your story nicely" and watched his poker face again, except for one thing. Back when I was with Bleys, before our attack on Amber, I had had a momentary contact with Brand while fooling with the Trumps. He had indicated distress, imprisonment, and then the contact had been broken. Random's story did fit, to that extent. So, instead, I said, "If he can point the finger, we have got to get him back and set him to pointing."

"I was hoping you would say that," Random replied.

"I hate to leave a bit of business like that unfinished."

I went and fetched the bottle, refilled our glasses. I sipped. I lit another cigarette.

"Before we get into that, though," I said, "I have to decide on the best way of breaking the news about Caine. Where is Flora, anyway?"

"Down in town, I think. She was here this morning. I can find her for you, I'm pretty sure."

"Do it, then. She is the only other one I know of who

has seen one of these guys, back when they broke into her place in Westchester. We might as well have her handy for that much corroboration as to their nastiness. Besides, I have some other things I want to ask her."

He swallowed his drink and rose.

"All right. I'll go do that now. Where should I bring her?"

"My quarters. If I'm not there, wait."

He nodded.

I rose and accompanied him into the hall.

"Have you got the key to this room?" I asked.

"It's on a hook inside."

"Better get it and lock up. We wouldn't want a premature unveiling."

He did that and gave me the key. I walked with him as far as the first landing and saw him on his way.

From my safe, I removed the Jewel of Judgment, a ruby pendant which had given Dad and Eric control over the weather in the vicinity of Amber. Before he died, Eric had told me the procedure to be followed in tuning it to my own use. I had not had time to do it, though, and did not really have the time now. But during my conversation with Random I had decided that I was going to have to take the time. I had located Dworkin's notes, beneath a stone near Eric's fireplace. He had given me that much information also, that last time. I would have liked to know where he had come across the notes in the first place, though, for they were incomplete. I fetched them from the rear of the safe and regarded them once again. They did agree with Eric's explanation as to how the attunement was to be managed.

But they also indicated that the stone had other uses, that the control of meteorological phenomena was almost an incidental, though spectacular, demonstration of a complex of principles which underlay the Pattern, the Trumps, and the physical integrity of Amber herself, apart from Shadow. Unfortunately, the details were lacking. Still, the more I searched my memory, the more something along these lines did seem indicated. Only rarely had Dad produced the stone; and though he had spoken of it as a weather changer, the weather had not always been especially altered on those occasions when he had sported it. And he had often taken it along with him on his little trips. So I was ready to believe that there was more to it than that. Eric had probably reasoned the same way, but he had not been able to dope out its other uses either. He had simply taken advantage of its obvious powers when Bleys and I had attacked Amber; and he had used it the same way this past week when the creatures had made their assault from the black road. It had served him well on both occasions, even if it had not been sufficient to save his life. So I had better get hold of its power myself, I decided, now. Any extra edge was important. And it would be good to be seen wearing the thing, too, I judged. Especially now.

I put the notes back into the safe, the jewel in my pocket. I left then and headed downstairs. Again, as before, to walk those halls made me feel as if I had never been away. This was home, this was what I wanted. Now I was its defender. I did not even wear the crown, yet all its problems had become my own. It was ironic. I had come back to claim the crown, to wrest it from Eric, to hold the glory, to reign. Now, suddenly, things were falling apart. It had not taken long to realize that Eric had behaved incorrectly. If he had indeed done Dad in, he had no right to the crown. If he had not, then he had acted prematurely. Either way, the coronation had served only to fatten his already obese ego. Myself, I wanted it and I knew that I could take it. But it would be equally irresponsible to do so with my troops quartered in Amber, suspicious of Caine's murder about to descend upon me, the first signs of a fantastic plot suddenly displayed before me, and the continuing possibility that Dad was still alive. On several occasions it seemed we had been in contact, briefly—and at one such time, years ago, that he had okayed my succession. But there was so much deceit and trickery afoot that I did not know what to believe. He had not abdicated. Also, I had had a head injury, and I was well aware of my own desires. The mind is a funny place. I do not even trust my own. Could it be that I had manufactured that whole business? A lot had happened since. The price of being an Amberite, I suppose, is that you cannot even trust yourself. I wondered what Freud would have said. While he had failed to pierce my amnesia, he had come up with some awfully good guesses as to what my father had been like, what our relationship had been, even though I had not realized it at the time. I wished that I could have one more session with him.

I made my way through the marble dining hall and into the dark, narrow corridor that lay behind. I nodded to the guard and walked on back to the door. Through it then, out onto the platform, across and down. The interminable spiral stairway that leads into the guts of Kolvir. Walking. Lights every now and then. Blackness beyond.

It seemed that a balance had shifted somewhere along the way, and that I was no longer acting but being acted upon, being forced to move, to respond. Being herded. And each move led to another. Where had it all begun? Maybe it had been going on for years and I was only just now becoming aware of it. Perhaps we were all victims, in a fashion and to a degree none of us had realized. Great victuals for morbid thought. Sigmund, where are you now? I had wanted to be king—still wanted to be king—more than anything else. Yet the more I learned and the more I thought about what I had learned, the more all of my movements actually seemed to amount to Amber Pawn to King Four. I realized then that this feeling had been present for some time, growing, and I did not like it at all. But nothing that has ever lived has gotten by without making some mistake, I consoled myself. If my feeling represented actuality, my personal Pavlov was getting closer to my fangs with each ringing of the bell. Soon now, soon, I felt that it had to be soon, I would have to see that he came very near. Then it would be mine to see that he neither went away nor ever came again.

Turning, turning, around and down, light here, light there, these my thoughts, like thread on a spool, winding or unwinding, hard to be sure. Below me the sound of metal against stone. A guard's scabbard, the guard rising. A ripple of light from a lantern raised.

"Lord Corwin . . ."

"Jamie."

At bottom, I took a lantern from the shelf. Putting a light to it, I turned and headed toward the tunnel, pushing the darkness on ahead of me, a step at a time.

Eventually the tunnel, and so up it, counting side passages. It was the seventh that I wanted. Echoes and shadows. Must and dust.

Coming to it, then. Turning there. Not too much farther.

Finally, that great, dark, metal-bound door. I unlocked it and pushed hard. It creaked, resisted, finally moved inward.

I set down the lantern, just to the right, inside. I had no further need of it, as the Pattern itself gave off sufficient light for what I had to do.

For a moment I regarded the Pattern—a shining mass of curved lines that tricked the eye as it tried to trace them—imbedded there, huge, in the floor's slick blackness. It had given me power over Shadow, it had restored most of my memory. It would also destroy me in an instant if I were to essay it improperly. What gratitude the prospect did arouse in me was therefore not untinged with fear. It was a splendid and cryptic old family heirloom which belonged right where it was, in the cellar.

I moved off to the corner where the tracery began. There I composed my mind, relaxed my body, and set my left foot upon the Pattern. Without pausing, I strode forward then and felt the current begin. Blue sparks outlined my boots. Another step. There was an audible crackling this time and the beginning of resistance. I took the first curvelength, striving to hurry, wanting to reach the First Veil as quickly as possible. By the time I did, my hair was stirring and the sparks were brighter, longer.

The strain increased. Each step required more effect than the previous one. The crackling grew louder and the current intensified. My hair rose and I shook off sparks. I kept my eyes on the fiery lines and did not stop pushing.

Suddenly the pressure abated. I staggered but kept moving. I was through the First Veil and into the feeling of accomplishment that that entailed. I recalled the last time that I had come this way, in Rebma, the city under the sea. The maneuver I had just completed was what had started the return of my memories. Yes. I pushed ahead and the sparks grew and the currents rose once again, setting my flesh to tingling.

The Second Veil . . . The angles . . . It always seemed to tax the strength to its limits, to produce the feeling that one's entire being was transformed into pure Will. It was a driving, relentless sensation. At the moment, the negotiation of the Pattern was the only thing in the world that meant anything to me. I had always been there, striving, never been away, always would be there, contending, my will against the maze of power. Time had vanished. Only the tension held.

The sparks were up to my waist. I entered the Grand Curve and fought my way along it. I was continually destroyed and reborn at every step of its length, baked by the fires of creation, chilled by the cold at entropy's end.

Out and onward, turning. Three more curves, a straight line, a number of arcs. Dizziness, a sensation of fading and intensifying as though I were oscillating into and out of existence. Turn after turn after turn after turn . . . A short, sharp arc . . . The line that led to the Final Veil . . . I imagine I was gasping and drenched with sweat by then. I never seem to remember for sure.

I could hardly move my feet. The sparks were up to my shoulders. They came into my eyes and I lost sight of the Pattern itself between blinks. In, out, in, out . . . There it was. I dragged my right foot forward, knowing how Benedict must have felt, his legs snared by the black grass. Right before I rabbit-punched him. I felt bludgeoned myself—all over. Left foot, forward . . . So slowly it was hard to be certain it was actually moving. My hands were blue flames, my legs pillars of fire. Another step. Another. Yet another.

I felt like a slowly animated statue, a thawing snowman, a buckling girder. . . . Two more . . . Three . . . Glacial, my movements, but I who directed them had all of eternity and a perfect constancy of will that would be realized. . . .

I passed through the Veil. A short arc followed. Three steps to cross it into blackness and peace. They were the worst of all.

A coffee break for Sisyphus! That was my first thought as I departed the Pattern. *I've done it again!* was my second. And, *Never again!* was my third.

I allowed myself the luxury of a few deep breaths and a little shaking. Then I unpocketed the jewel and raised it by its chain. I held it before my eye.

Red inside, of course—a deep cherry-red, smokeshot, fulgent. It seemed to have picked up something extra of light and glitter during the trip through the Pattern. I continued to stare, thinking over the instructions, comparing them with things I already knew.

Once you have walked the Pattern and reached this point, you can cause it to transport you to any place that you can visualize. All that it takes is the desire and an act of will. Such being the case, I was not without a moment's trepidation. If the effect proceeded as it normally did, I could be throwing myself into a peculiar sort of trap. But Eric had succeeded. He had not been locked into the heart of a gem somewhere off in Shadow. The Dworkin who had written those notes had been a great man, and I had trusted him.

Composing my mind, I intensified my security of the stone's interior.

There was a distorted reflection of the Pattern within it, surrounded by winking points of light, tiny flares and flashes, different curves and paths. I made my decision, I focused my will. . . .

Redness and slow motion. Like sinking into an ocean of high viscosity. Very slowly, at first. Drifting and darkening, all the pretty lights far, far ahead. Faintly, my apparent velocity increased. Flakes of light, distant, intermittent. A trifle faster then, it seemed. No scale. I was a point of consciousness of indeterminate dimensions. Aware of movement, aware of the configuration toward which I advanced, now almost rapidly. The redness was nearly gone, as was the consciousness of any medium. Resistance vanished. I was speeding. All of this, now, seemed to have taken but a single instant, was still taking that same instant. There was a peculiar, timeless quality to the entire affair. My velocity relative to what now seemed my target was enormous. The little, twisted maze was growing, was resolving into what appeared a three-dimensional variation of the Pattern itself. Punctuated by flares of colored light, it grew before me, still reminiscent of a bizarre galaxy half raveled in the middle of the ever-night, haloed with a pale shine of dust, its streamers composed of countless flickering points. And it grew or I shrank, or it advanced or I advanced, and we were near, near together, and it filled all of space now, top to bottom, this way to that, and my personal velocity still seemed, if anything, to be increasing. I was caught, overwhelmed by the blaze, and there was a stray streamer which I knew to be the beginning. I was too close—lost, actually—to apprehend its over-all configuration any longer, but the buckling, the flickering, the weaving of all that I could see of it, everywhere about me, made me wonder whether three dimensions were sufficient to account for the senses-warping complexities with which I was confronted. Rather than my galactic analogy, something in my mind

shifted to the other extreme, suggesting the infinitely
dimensioned Hilbert space of the subatomic. But then,
it was a metaphor of desperation. Truly and simply, I
did not understand anything about it. I had only a growing feeling—Pattern-conditioned? Instinctive?—that I
had to pass through this maze also to gain the new
degree of power that I sought.

Nor was I incorrect. I was swept on into it without
any slackening of my apparent velocity. I was spun and
whirled along blazing ways, passing through substance-
less clouds of glitter and shine. There were no areas of
resistance, as in the Pattern itself, my initial impetus
seeming sufficient to bear me throughout. A whirlwind
tour of the Milky Way? A drowning man swept among
canyons of coral? An insomniac sparrow passing over
an amusement park of a July Fourth evening? These
my thoughts as I recapitulated my recent passage in this
transformed fashion.

. . . And out, through, over, and done, in a blaze of
ruddy light that found me regarding myself holding the
pendant beside the Pattern, then regarding the pendant,
Pattern within it, within me, everything within me, me
within it, the redness subsiding, down, gone. Then just
me, the pendant, the Pattern, alone, subject-object relationships reestablished—only an octave higher, which I
feel is about the best way there is to put it. For a
certain empathy now existed. It was as though I had
acquired an extra sense, and an additional means of
expression. It was a peculiar sensation, satisfying.

Anxious to test it, I summoned my resolve once again
and commanded the Pattern to transport me elsewhere.

I stood then in the round room, atop the highest
tower in Amber. Crossing it, I passed outside, onto a
very small balcony. The contrast was powerful, coming
so close to the supersensory voyage I had just completed. For several long moments I simply stood there,
looking.

The sea was a study in textures, as the sky was partly
overcast and getting on toward evening. The clouds

themselves showed patterns of soft brightness and rough shading. The wind made its way seaward, so that the salt smell was temporarily denied me. Dark birds dotted the air, swinging and hovering at a great distance out over the water. Below me, the palace yards and the terraces of the city lay spread in enduring elegance out to Kolvir's rim. People were tiny on the thoroughfares, their movements discountable. I felt very alone.

Then I touched the pendant and called for a storm.

Random and Flora were waiting in my quarters when I returned. Random's eyes went first to the pendant, then to my own. I nodded.

I turned toward Flora, bowing slightly.

"Sister," I said, "it has been a while, and then a while."

She looked somewhat frightened, which was all to the good. She smiled and took my hand, though.

"Brother," she said. "I see that you have kept your word."

Pale gold, her hair. She had cut it, but retained the bangs. I could not decide whether I liked it that way or not. She had very lovely hair. Blue eyes, too, and tons of vanity to keep everything in her favorite perspective. At times she seemed to behave quite stupidly, but then at other times I have wondered.

"Excuse me for staring," I said, "but the last time that we met I was unable to see you."

"I am very happy that the situation has been corrected," she said. "It was quite— There was nothing that I could do, you know."

"I know," I said, recalling the occasional lilt of her laughter from the other side of the darkness on one of the anniversaries of the event. "I know."

I moved to the window and opened it, knowing that the rain would not be coming in. I like the smell of a storm.

"Random, did you learn anything of interest with regard to a possible postman?" I asked.

"Not really," he said. "I made some inquiries. No one seems to have seen anyone else in the right place at the right time."

"I see," I said. "Thank you. I may see you again later."

"All right," he said. "I'll be in my quarters all evening, then."

I nodded, turned, leaned back against the sill, watched Flora. Random closed the door quietly as he left. I listened to the rain for half a minute or so.

"What are you going to do with me?" she said finally.

"Do?"

"You are in a position to call for a settlement on old debts. I assume that things are about to begin."

"Perhaps," I said. "Most things depend on other things. This thing is no different."

"What do you mean?"

"Give me what I want, and we'll see. I have even been known to be a nice guy on occasion."

"What is it that you want?"

"The story, Flora. Let's start with that. Of how you came to be my shepherdess there on that shadow, Earth. All pertinent details. What was the arrangement? What was the understanding? Everything. That's all."

She sighed.

"The beginning . . ." she said. "Yes . . . It was in Paris, a party, at a certain Monsieur Focault's. This was about three years before the Terror—"

"Stop," I said. "What were you doing there?"

"I had been in that general area of Shadow for approximately five of their years," she said. "I had been wandering, looking for something novel, something that suited my fancy. I came upon that place at that time in the same way we find anything. I let my desires lead me and I followed my instincts."

"A peculiar coincidence."

"Not in light of all the time involved—and considering the amount of travel in which we indulge. It was, if you like, my Avalon, my Amber surrogate, my home away from home. Call it what you will, I was there, at that party, that October night, when you came in with the little redheaded girl—Jacqueline, I believe, was her name."

That brought it back, from quite a distance, a memory I hadn't called for in a long, long while. I remembered Jacqueline far better than I did Focault's party, but there had been such an occasion.

"Go ahead."

"As I said," she went on, "I was there. You arrived later. You caught my attention immediately, of course. Still, if one exists for a sufficiently long period of time and travels considerably, one does occasionally encounter a person greatly resembling someone else one has known. That was my first thought after the initial excitement faded. Surely it had to be a double. So much time had passed without a whisper. Yet we all have secrets and good reasons for having them. This could be one of yours. So I saw that we were introduced and then had a devil of a time getting you away from that little redheaded piece for more than a few minutes. And you insisted your name was Fenneval——Cordell Fenneval. I grew uncertain. I could not tell whether it was a double or you playing games. The third possibility did cross my mind, though—that you had dwelled in some adjacent area of Shadow for a sufficient time to cast shadows of yourself. I might have departed still wondering had not Jacqueline later boasted to me concerning your strength. Now this is not the commonest subject of conversation for a woman, and the way in which she said it led me to believe that she had actually been quite impressed by some things you had done. I drew her out a bit and realized that they were all of them feats of which you were capable. That eliminated the notion of it being a double. It had to be either you or your shadow. This in mind, even if Cordell was not Corwin he was a clue, a clue that you were or had been in that shady neighborhood—the first real clue I had come across concerning your whereabouts. I had to pursue it. I began keeping track of you then, checking into your past. The more people I questioned, the more puzzling it became. In fact, after several months I was still unable to decide. There were enough smudgy areas to make it possible. Things were resolved for me the following summer, though, when I revisited Amber for a time. I mentioned the peculiar affair to Eric . . ."

"Yes?"

"Well . . . he was—somewhat—aware—of the possibility."

She paused and rearranged her gloves on the seat beside her.

"Uh-huh," I said. "Just what did he tell you?"

"That it might be the real you," she said. "He told me there had been—an accident."

"Really?"

"Well, no," she admitted. "Not an accident. He said there had been a fight and he had injured you. He thought you were going to die, and he did not want the blame. So he transported you off into Shadow and left you there, in that place. After a long while, he decided that you must be dead, that it was finally all over between you. My news naturally disturbed him. So he swore me to secrecy and sent me back to keep you under surveillance. I had a good excuse for being there, as I had already told everyone how much I liked the place."

"You didn't promise to keep silent for nothing, Flora. What did he give you?"

"He gave me his word that should he ever come into power here in Amber, I would not be forgotten."

"A little risky," I said. "After all, that would still leave you with something on him—knowledge of the whereabouts of a rival claimant, and of his part in putting him there."

"True. But things sort of balanced out, and I would have to admit having become an accomplice in order to talk about it."

I nodded.

"Tight, but not impossible," I agreed. "But did you think he would let me continue living if he ever did get a chance at the throne?"

"That was never discussed. Never."

"It must have crossed your mind, though."

"Yes, later," she said, "and I decided that he would probably do nothing. After all, it was beginning to seem likely that you had been deprived of your memory. There was no reason to do anything to you so long as you were harmless."

"So you stayed on to watch me, to see that I remained harmless?"

"Yes."

"What would you have done had I shown signs of recovering my memory?"

She looked at me, then looked away.

"I would have reported it to Eric."

"And what would he have done then?"

"I don't know."

I laughed a little, and she blushed. I could not remember the last time I had seen Flora blush.

"I will not belabor the obvious," I said. "All right, you stayed on, you watched me. What next? What happened?"

"Nothing special. You just went on leading your life and I went on keeping track of it."

"All of the others knew where you were?"

"Yes. I'd make no secret of my whereabouts. In fact, all of them came around to visit me at one time or another."

"That includes Random?"

She curled her lip.

"Yes, several times," she said.

"Why the sneer?"

"It is too late to start pretending I like him," she said. "You know. I just don't like the people he associates with—assorted criminals, jazz musicians. . . . I had to show him family courtesy when he was visiting my shadow, but he put a big strain on my nerves, bringing those people around at all hours—jam sessions, poker parties. The place usually reeked for weeks afterward and I was always glad to see him go. Sorry. I know you like him, but you wanted the truth."

"He offended your delicate sensibilities. Okay. I now direct your attention to the brief time when I was your guest. Random joined us rather abruptly. Pursuing him were half a dozen nasty fellows whom we dispatched in your living room.'

"I recall the event quite vividly."

"Do you recall the guys responsible—the creatures we had to deal with?"

"Yes."

"Sufficiently well to recognize one if you ever saw another?"

"I think so."

"Good. Had you ever seen one before?"

"No."

"Since?"

"No."

"Had you ever heard them described anywhere?"

"Not that I can remember. Why?"

I shook my head.

"Not yet. This is my inquisition, remember? Now I want you to think back for a time before that evening. Back to the event that put me in Greenwood. Maybe even a little earlier. What happened, and how did you find out about it? What were the circumstances? What was your part in things?"

"Yes," she said. "I knew you would ask me that sooner or later. What happened was that Eric contacted me the day after it occurred—from Amber, via my Trump." She glanced at me again, obviously to see how I was taking it, to study my reactions. I remained expressionless. "He told me you had been in a bad accident the previous evening, and that you were hospitalized. He told me to have you transferred to a private place, one where I could have more say as to the course of your treatment."

"In other words, he wanted me to stay a vegetable."

"He wanted them to keep you sedated."

"Did he or did he not admit to being responsible for the accident?"

"He did not say that he had had someone shoot out your tire, but he did know that that was what had happened. How else could he have known? When I learned later that he was planning to take the throne, I assumed that he had finally decided it was best to remove you entirely. When the attempt failed, it seemed logical that he would do the next most effective thing: see that you were kept out of the way until after the coronation."

"I was not aware that the tire had been shot out," I said.

Her face changed. She recovered.

"You told me that you knew it was not an accident —that someone had tried to kill you. I assumed you were aware of the specifics."

I was treading on slightly mucky ground again for the first time in a long while. I still had a bit of amnesia, and I had decided I probably always would. My memories of the few days prior to the accident were still spotty. The Pattern had restored the lost memories of my entire life up until then, but the trauma appeared to have destroyed recollection of some of the events immediately preceding it. Not an uncommon occurrence. Organic damage rather than simple functional distress, most likely. I was happy enough to have all the rest back, so those did not seem especially lamentable. As to the accident itself, and my feelings that it had been more than an accident, I did recall the gunshots. There had been two of them. I might even have glimpsed the figure with the rifle—fleetingly, too late. Or maybe that was pure fantasy. It seemed that I had, though. I had had something like that in mind when I had headed out for Westchester. Even at this late time, though, when

I held the power in Amber, I was loath to admit this single deficiency. I had faked my way with Flora before with a lot less to go on. I decided to stick with a winning combination.

"I was in no position to get out and see what had been hit," I said. "I heard the shots. I lost control. I had assumed that it was a tire, but I never knew for sure. The only reason I raised the question was because I was curious as to how you knew it was a tire."

"I already told you that Eric told me about it."

"It was the way that you said it that bothered me. You made it sound as if you already knew all the details before he contacted you."

She shook her head.

"Then pardon my syntax," she said. "That sometimes happens when you look at things after the fact. I am going to have to deny what you are implying. I had nothing to do with it and I had no prior knowledge that it had occurred."

"Since Eric is no longer around to confirm or deny anything, we will simply have to let it go," I said, "for now," and I said it to make her look even harder to her defense, to direct her attention away from any possible slip, either in word or expression, from which she might infer the small flaw which still existed in my memory. "Did you later become aware of the identity of the person with the gun?" I asked.

"Never," she said. "Most likely some hired thug. I don't know."

"Have you any idea how long I was unconscious before someone found me, took me to a hospital?"

She shook her head again.

Something was bothering me and I could not quite put my finger on it.

"Did Eric say what time I had been taken into the hospital?"

"No."

"When I was with you, why did you try walking back to Amber rather than using Eric's Trump?"

"I couldn't raise him."

"You could have called someone else to bring you through," I said. "Flora, I think you are lying to me."

It was really only a test, to observe her reaction. Why not?

"About what?" she asked. "I couldn't raise anyone else. They were all otherwise occupied. Is that what you mean?"

She studied me.

I raised my arm and pointed at her and the lightning flashed at my back, just outside the window. I felt a tingle, a mild jolt. The thunderclap was also impressive.

"You sin by omission," I tried.

She covered her face with her hands and began to weep.

"I don't know what you mean!" she said. "I answered all your questions! What do you want? I don't know where you were going or who shot at you or what time it occurred! I just know the facts I've given you, damn it!"

She was either sincere or unbreakable by these means, I decided. Whichever, I was wasting my time and could get nothing more this way. Also, I had better switch us away from the accident before she began thinking too much about its importance to me. If there was something there that I was missing, I wanted to find it first.

"Come with me," I said.

"Where are we going?"

"I have something I want you to identify. I will tell you why after you see it."

She rose and followed me. I took her up the hall to see the body before I gave her the story on Caine. She regarded the corpse quite dispassionately. She nodded.

"Yes," she said, and, "Even if I did not know it I would be glad to say that I did, for you."

I grunted a noncommittal. Family loyalty always touches me, somewhere. I could not tell whether she believed what I had said about Caine. But things sort of equal to equal things sort of being equal to each other, it didn't much seem to matter. I did not tell her anything about Brand and she did not seem to possess any new information concerning him. Her only other comment when everything I'd had to say was said, was, "You wear the jewel well. What about the headpiece?"

"It is too soon to talk of such things," I told her.

"Whatever my support may be worth . . ."

"I know," I said. "I know."

My tomb is a quiet place. It stands alone in a rocky declivity, shielded on three sides against the elements, surrounded by transported soil wherein a pair of scrubby trees, miscellaneous shrubs, weeds, and great ropes of mountain ivy are rooted, about two miles down, in back of the crest of Kolvir. It is a long, low building with two benches in front, and the ivy has contrived to cover it to a great extent, mercifully masking most of a bombastic statement graven on its face beneath my name. It is, understandably, vacant most of the time.

That evening, however, Ganelon and I repaired thither, accompanied by a good supply of wine and some loaves and cold cuts.

"You weren't joking!" he said, having dismounted, crossed over, and parted the ivy, able to read by the moon's light the words that were rendered there.

"Of course not," I said, climbing down and taking charge of the horses. "It's mine all right."

Tethering our mounts to a nearby shrub, I unslung our bags of provisions and carried them to the nearest bench. Ganelon joined me as I opened the first bottle and poured us a dark, deep pair.

"I still don't understand," he said, accepting his.

"What's there to understand? I'm dead and buried there," I said. "It's my cenotaph, is what it is—the monument that gets set up when the body has not been recovered. I only just learned about mine recently. It was raised several centuries ago, when it was decided I wasn't coming back."

"Kind of spooky," he said. "What's inside then?"

"Nothing. Though they did thoughtfully provide a niche and a casket, just in case my remains put in an appearance. You cover both bets that way."

Ganelon made himself a sandwich.

"Whose idea was it?" he asked.

"Random thinks it was Brand's or Eric's. No one remembers for sure. They all seemed to feel it was a good idea at the time."

He chuckled, an evil noise that perfectly suited his creased, scarred, and red-bearded self.

"What's to become of it now?"

I shrugged.

"I suppose some of them think it's a shame to waste it this way and would like to see me fill it. In the meantime, though, it's a good place to come and get drunk. I hadn't really paid my respects yet. "

I put together a pair of sandwiches and ate them both. This was the first real breather I had had since my return, and perhaps the last for some time to come. It was impossible to say. But I had not really had a chance to speak with Ganelon at any length during the past week, and he was one of the few persons I trusted. I wanted to tell him everything. I had to. I had to talk with someone who was not a part of it in the same way as the rest of us. So I did.

The moon moved a considerable distance and the shards of broken glass multiplied within my crypt.

"So how did the others take it?" he asked me.

"Predictably," I answered. "I could tell that Julian did not believe a word of it even though he said that he did. He knows how I feel about him, and he is in no position to challenge me. I don't think Benedict believes me either, but he is a lot harder to read. He is biding his time, and I hope giving me the benefit of the doubt while he is about it. As for Gérard, I have the feeling that this was the final weight, and whatever trust he had left for me has just collapsed. Still, he will be returning to Amber early tomorrow, to accompany me to the grove to recover Caine's body. No sense in turning it into a safari, but I did want another family member present. Deirdre now—she seemed happy about it. Didn't believe a word, I'm sure. But no matter. She has always been on my side, and she has never liked Caine. I'd say she is glad that I seem to be consolidating my position. I can't really tell whether Llewella believed me or not. She doesn't much give a damn what the rest of us do to one another, so far as I can see. As to Fiona, she simply seemed amused at the whole business. But then, she has always had this detached, superior way of regarding things. You can never be certain what represents her real thinking."

"Did you tell them the business about Brand yet?"

"No. I told them about Caine and I told them I wanted them all to be in Amber by tomorrow evening. That is when the subject of Brand will be raised. I've an idea I want to try out."

"You contacted all of them by means of the Trumps?"

"That's right."

"There is something I have been meaning to ask you about that. Back on the shadow world we visited to obtain the weapons, there are telephones. . . ."

"Yes?"

"I learned about wiretaps and such while we were there. Is it possible, do you think, that the Trumps could be bugged?"

I began to laugh, then caught myself as some of the implications of his suggestion sank in. Finally, "I don't really know," I said. "So much concerning Dworkin's work remains a mystery—the thought just never occurred to me. I've never tried it myself. I wonder, though. . . ."

"Do you know how many sets there are?"

"Well, everyone in the family has a pack or two and there were a dozen or so spares in the library. I don't really know whether there are any others."

"It seems to me that a lot could be learned just by listening in."

"Yes. Dad's deck, Brand's, my original pack, the one

Random lost— Hell! There are quite a number unaccounted for these days. I don't know what to do about it. Start an inventory and try some experiments, I guess. Thanks for mentioning it."

He nodded and we both sipped for a while in silence. Then, "What are you going to do, Corwin?" he asked.

"About what?"

"About everything. What do we attack now, and in what order?"

"My original intention was to begin tracing the black road toward its origin as soon as things were more settled here in Amber," I said. "Now, though, I have shifted my priorities. I want Brand returned as soon as possible, if he is still living. If not, I want to find out what happened to him."

"But will the enemy give you the breathing time? He might be preparing a new offensive right now."

"Yes, of course. I have considered that. I feel we have some time, since they were defeated so recently. They will have to pull themselves together again, beef up their forces, reassess the situation in light of our new weapons. What I have in mind for the moment is to establish a series of lookout stations along the road to give us advance warning of any new movements on their part. Benedict has already agreed to take charge of the operation."

"I wonder how much time we have."

I poured him another drink, as it was the only answer I could think of.

"Things were never this complicated back in Avalon —*our* Avalon, I mean."

"True," I said. "You are not the only one who misses those days. At least, they seem simpler now."

He nodded. I offered him a cigarette, but he declined in favor of his pipe. In the flamelight, he studied the Jewel of Judgment which still hung about my neck.

"You say you can really control the weather with that thing?" he asked.

"Yes," I said.

"How do you know?"

"I've tried it. It works."

"What did you do?"

"That storm this afternoon. It was mine."

"I wonder . . ."

"What?"

"I wonder what I would have done with that sort of power. What I would do with it."

"The first thing that crossed my mind," I said, slapping the wall of my tomb, "was to destroy this place by lightning—strike it repeatedly and reduce it to rubble. Leave no doubt in anyone's mind as to my feelings, my power."

"Why didn't you?"

"Got to thinking about it a bit more then. Decided— Hell! They might really have a use for the place before too long, if I'm not smart enough or tough enough or lucky enough. Such being the case, I tried to decide where I would like them to dump my bones. It caught me then that this is really a pretty good spot— up high, clean, where the elements still walk naked. Nothing in sight but rock and sky. Stars, clouds, sun, moon, wind, rain , . . better company than a lot of other stiffs. Don't know why I should have to lie beside anyone I wouldn't want next to me now, and there aren't many."

"You're getting morbid, Corwin. Or drunk. Or both. Bitter, too. You don't need that."

"Who the hell are you to say what I need?"

I felt him stiffen beside me, then relax.

"I don't know," he finally said. "Just saying what I see."

"How are the troops holding up?" I asked.

"I think they are still bewildered, Corwin. They came to fight a holy war on the slopes of heaven. They think that's what the shooting was all about last week. So they are happy on that count, seeing as we won. But now this waiting, in the city . . . They don't understand the place. Some of the ones they thought to be enemies are now friends. They are confused. They know they are being kept ready for combat, but they have no idea against whom, or when. As they have been restricted to the billets the whole time, they have not yet realized the extent to which their presence is resented by the regulars and the population at large. They will probably be catching on fairly soon, though. I had been waiting to raise the subject, but you've been so busy lately. . . ."

I sat smoking for a time.

Then, "I guess I had better have a talk with them," I said. "Won't have a chance tomorrow, though, and something should be done soon. I think they should be moved—to a bivouac area in the Forest of Arden. Tomorrow, yes. I'll locate it for you on the map when we get back. Tell them it is to keep them close to the black road. Tell them that another attack could come that way at any time—which is no less than the truth. Drill them, maintain their fighting edge. I'll come down as soon as I can and talk to them."

"That will leave you without a personal force in Amber."

"True. It may prove a useful risk, though, both as a demonstration of confidence and a gesture of consideration. Yes, I think it will turn out to be a good move. If not . . ." I shrugged.

I poured and tossed another empty into my tomb.

"By the way," I said, "I'm sorry."

"What for?"

"I just noticed that I am morbid and drunk and bitter. I don't need that."

He chuckled and clicked his glass against my own.

"I know," he said. "I know."

So we sat there while the moon fell, till the last bottle was interred among its fellows. We talked for a time of days gone by. At length we fell silent and my eyes drifted to the stars above Amber. It was good that we had come to this place, but now the city was calling me back. Knowing my thoughts, Ganclon rose and stretched, headed for the horses. I relieved myself beside my tomb and followed him.

5

The Grove of the Unicorn lies in Arden to the south-west of Kolvir, near to that jutting place where the land begins its final descent into the valley called Garnath. While Garnath had been cursed, burned, invaded, and fought through in recent years, the adjacent highlands stood unmolested. The grove where Dad claimed to have seen the unicorn ages before and to have experienced the peculiar events which led to his adopting the beast as the patron of Amber and placing it on his coat of arms, was, as near as we could tell, a spot now but slightly screened from the long view across Garnath to the sea—twenty or thirty paces in from the upper edge of things: an asymmetrical glade where a small spring trickled from a mass of rock, formed a clear pool, brimmed into a tiny creek, made its way off toward Garnath and on down.

It was to this place that Gérard and I rode the following day, leaving at an hour that found us halfway down our trail from Kolvir before the sun skipped flakes of light across the ocean, then cast its whole bucketful against the sky. Gérard drew rein as it was doing this. He dismounted then and motioned to me to do the same. I did, leaving Star and the pack horse I was leading there beside his own huge piebald. I followed him off perhaps a dozen paces into a basin half-filled with gravel. He halted and I came up beside him.

"What is it?" I asked.

He turned and faced me and his eyes were narrow and his jaw clamped tight. He unfastened his cloak, folded it, and placed it on the ground. He unclapped his swordbelt and lay it atop the cloak.

"Get rid of your blade and your cloak," he said. "They will only get in the way."

I had an inkling of what was coming, and I decided I had better go along with it. I folded my cloak, placed the Jewel of Judgment beside Grayswandir, and faced him once again. I said only one word.

"Why?"

"It has been a long time," he said, "and you might have forgotten."

He came at me slowly, and I got my arms out in front of me and backed away. He did not swing at me. I used to be faster than he was. We were both crouched, and he was making slow, pawing movements with his left hand, his right hand nearer to his body, twitching slightly.

If I had had to choose a place to fight with Gérard, this would not have been it. He, of course, was aware of this. If I had to fight with Gérard at all, I would not have chosen to do so with my hands. I am better than Gérard with a blade or a quarterstaff. Anything that involved speed and strategy and gave me a chance to hit him occasionally while keeping him at bay would permit me to wear him down eventually and provide openings for heavier and heavier assaults. He, of course, was aware of this also. That is why he had trapped me as he had. I understood Gérard, though, and I had to play by his rules now.

I brushed his hand away a couple of times as he stepped up his movements, pressing nearer to me with every pace. Finally I took a chance, ducked and swung. I landed a fast, hard left just a little above his middle. It would have broken a stout board or ruptured the insides of a lesser mortal. Unfortunately, time had not softened Gérard. I heard him grunt, but he blocked my right, got his right hand under my left arm, and caught my shoulder from behind.

I closed with him fast then, anticipating a shoulder

lock I might not be able to break; and, turning, driving forward, catching his left shoulder in a similar fashion, I hooked my right leg behind his knee and was able to cast him backward to the ground.

He maintained his grip, though, and I came down atop him. I released my own hold and was able to drive my right elbow into his left side as we hit. The angle was not ideal and his left hand went up and across, reaching to grasp his right somewhere behind my head.

I was able to duck out of it, but he still had my arm. For a moment I had a clear shot at his groin with my right, but I restrained myself. It is not that I have any qualms about hitting a man below his belt. I knew that if I did it to Gérard just then his reflexes would probably cause him to break my shoulder. Instead, scraping my forearm on the gravel, I managed to twist my left arm up behind his head, while at the same time sliding my right arm between his legs and catching him about the left thigh. I rolled back as I did this, attempting to straighten my legs as soon as my feet were beneath me. I wanted to raise him off the ground and slam him down again, driving my shoulder into his middle for good measure.

But Gérard scissored his legs and rolled to the left, forcing me to somersault across his body. I let go my hold on his head and pulled my left arm free as I went over. I scrambled clockwise then, dragging my right arm away and going for a toehold.

But Gérard would have none of that. He had gotten his arms beneath him by then. With one great heave he tore himself free and twisted his way back to his feet. I straightened myself and leaped backwards. He began moving toward me immediately, and I decided that he was going to maul the hell out of me if I just kept grappling with him. I had to take a few chances.

I watched his feet, and at what I judged to be the best moment I dove in beneath his extended arms just as he was shifting his weight forward onto his left foot and raising his right. I was able to catch hold of his

right ankle and hoist it about four feet high behind him.
He went over and down, forward and to his left.

He scrambled to get to his feet and I caught him on
the jaw with a left that knocked him down again. He
shook his head and blocked with his arms as he came
up once more. I tried to kick him in the stomach, but
missed as he pivoted, catching him on the hip. He
maintained his balance and advanced again.

I threw jabs at his face and circled. I caught him
twice more in the stomach and danced away. He smiled.
He knew I was afraid to close with him. I snapped a
kick at his stomach and connected. His arms dropped
sufficiently for me to chop him alongside the neck,
just above the collarbone. At that moment, however,
his arms shot forward and locked about my waist. I
slammed his jaw with the heel of my hand, but it did
not stop him from tightening his grip and raising me
above the ground. Too late to hit him again. Those
massive arms were already crushing my kidneys. I
sought his carotids with my thumbs, squeezed.

But he kept raising me, back, up over his head.
My grip loosened, slipped away. Then he slammed
me down on my back in the gravel, as peasant women
do their laundry on rocks.

There were exploding points of light and the world
was a jittering, half-real place as he dragged me to
my feet again. I saw his fist—

The sunrise was lovely, but the angle was wrong. . .
By about ninety degrees . . .

Suddenly I was assailed by vertigo. It canceled out
the beginning awareness of a roadmap of pains that
ran along my back and reached the big city somewhere
in the vicinity of my chin.

I was hanging high in the air. By turning my head
slightly I could see for a very great distance, down.

I felt a set of powerful clamps affixed to my body—
shoulder and thigh. When I turned to look at them,
I saw that they were hands. Twisting my neck even

farther, I saw that they were Gérard's hands. He was
holding me at full arm's length above his head. He
stood at the very edge of the trail, and I could see
Garnath and the terminus of the black road far below.
If he let go, part of me might join the bird droppings
that smeared the cliff face and the rest would come to
resemble washed-up jellyfish I had known on beaches
past.

"Yes. Look down, Corwin," he said, feeling me stir,
glancing up, meeting my eyes. "All that I need to do
is open my hands."

"I hear you," I said softly, trying to figure a way to
drag him along with me if he decided to do it.

"I am not a clever man," he said. "But I had a
thought—a terrible thought. This is the only way that
I know to do something about it. My thought was that
you had been away from Amber for an awfully long
while. I have no way of knowing whether the story
about your losing your memory is entirely true. You
have come back and you have taken charge of things,
but you do not yet truly rule here. I was troubled by
the deaths of Benedict's servants, as I am troubled
now by the death of Caine. But Eric has died recently
also, and Benedict is maimed. It is not so easy to
blame you for this part of things, but it has occurred
to me that it might be possible—if it should be that
you are secretly allied with our enemies of the black
road."

"I am not," I said.

"It does not matter, for what I have to say," he
said. "Just hear me out. Things will go the way that
they will go. If, during your long absence, you arranged this state of affairs—possibly even removing
Dad and Brand as part of your design—then I see
you as out to destroy all family resistance to your
usurpation."

"Would I have delivered myself to Eric to be
blinded and imprisoned if this were the case?"

"Hear me out!" he repeated. "You could easily have

made mistakes that led to that. It does not matter now. You may be as innocent as you say or as guilty as possible. Look down, Corwin. That is all. Look down at the black road. Death is the limit of the distance you travel if that is your doing. I have shown you my strength once again, lest you have forgotten. I can kill you, Corwin. Do not even be certain that your blade will protect you, if I can get my hands on you but once. And I will, to keep my promise. My promise is only that if you are guilty I will kill you the moment I learn of it. Know also that my life is insured, Corwin, for it is linked now to your own."

"What do you mean?"

"All of the others are with us at this moment, via my Trump, watching, listening. You cannot arrange my removal now without revealing your intentions to the entire family. That way, if I die forsworn, my promise can still be kept."

"I get the point," I said. "And if someone else kills you? They remove me, also. That leaves Julian, Benedict, Random, and the girls to man the barricades. Better and better—for whoever it is. Whose idea was this, really?"

"Mine! Mine alone!" he said, and I felt his grip tighten, his arms bend and grow tense. "You are just trying to confuse things! Like you always do!" he groaned. "Things didn't go bad till you came back! Damn it, Corwin! I think it's your fault!"

Then he hurled me into the air.

"Not guilty, Gérard!" was all I had time to shout.

Then he caught me—a great, shoulder-wrenching grab—and snatched me back from the precipice. He swung me in and around and set me on my feet. He walked off immediately, heading back to the gravelly area where we had fought. I followed him and we collected our things.

As he was clasping his big belt he looked up at me and looked away again.

"We'll not talk about it any more," he said.

"All right."

I turned and walked back to the horses. We mounted and continued on down the trail.

The spring made its small music in the grove. Higher now, the sun strung lines of light through the trees. There was still some dew on the ground. The sod that I had cut for Caine's grave was moist with it.

I fetched the spade that I had packed and opened the grave. Without a word, Gérard helped me move the body onto a piece of sailcloth we had brought for that purpose. We folded it about him and closed it with big, loose stitches.

"Corwin! Look!" It was a whisper, and Gérard's hand closed on my elbow as he spoke.

I followed the direction of his gaze and froze. Neither of us moved as we regarded the apparition: a soft, shimmering white encompassed it, as if it were covered with down rather than fur and maning; its tiny, cloven hooves were golden, as was the delicate, whorled horn that rose from its narrow head. It stood atop one of the lesser rocks, nibbling at the lichen that grew there. Its eyes, when it raised them and looked in our direction, were a bright, emerald green. It joined us in immobility for a pair of instants. Then it made a quick, nervous gesture with its front feet, pawing the air and striking the stone, three times. And then it blurred and vanished like a snowflake, silently, perhaps in the woods to our right.

I rose and crossed to the stone. Gérard followed me. There, in the moss, I traced its tiny hoofmarks.

"Then we really did see it," Gérard said.

I nodded.

"We saw something. Did you ever see it before?"

"No. Did you?"

I shook my head.

"Julian claims he once saw it," he said, "in the distance. Says his hounds refused to give chase."

"It was beautiful. That long, silky tail, those shiny hooves . . ."

"Yes. Dad always took it as a good omen."

"I'd like to myself."

"Strange time for it to appear . . . All these years . . ."

I nodded again.

"Is there a special observance? It being our patron and all . . . is there something we should do?"

"If there is, Dad never told me about it," I said. I patted the rock on which it had appeared. "If you herald some turn in our fortunes, if you bring us some measure of grace—thanks, unicorn," I said. "And even if you do not, thanks for the brightness of your company at a dark time."

We went and drank from the spring then. We secured our grim parcel on the back of the third horse. We led our mounts until we were away from the place, where, save for the water, things had become very still.

Life's incessant ceremonies leap everlasting, humans spring eternal on hope's breast, and frying pans without fires are often far between: the sum of my long life's wisdom that evening, tendered in a spirit of creative anxiety, answered by Random with a nod and a friendly obscenity.

We were in the library, and I was seated on the edge of the big desk. Random occupied a chair to my right. Gérard stood at the other end of the room, inspecting some weapons that hung on the wall. Or maybe it was Rein's etching of the unicorn he was looking at. Whichever, along with ourselves, he was also ignoring Julian, who was slouched in an easy chair beside the display cases, right center, legs extended and crossed at the ankles, arms folded, staring down at his scaley boots. Fiona—five-two, perhaps, in height—green eyes fixed on Flora's own blue as they spoke, there beside the fireplace, hair more than compensating for the vacant hearth, smoldering, reminded me, as always, of something from which the artist had just drawn back, setting aside his tools, questions slowly forming behind his smile. The place at the base of her throat where his thumb had notched the collarbone always drew my eyes as the mark of a master craftsman, especially when she raised her head, quizzical or imperious, to regard us taller others. She smiled faintly, just then, doubtless aware of my gaze, an almost clairvoyant faculty the acceptance of which has never deprived of its ability to disconcert. Llewella, off in a corner, pretending to study a book, had her back to the rest of us, her green tresses bobbed a couple of inches above her dark collar. Whether her withdrawal involved animus, self-conscious in her alienation, or simple caution, I could never be certain. Probably something of all these. Hers was not that familiar a presence in Amber.

. . . And the fact that we constituted a collection of individuals rather than a group, a family, at a time when I wanted to achieve some over-identity, some will to cooperate, was what led to my observations and Random's acknowledgement.

I felt a familiar presence, heard a "Hello, Corwin" and there was Deirdre, reaching toward me. I extended my hand, clasped her own, raised it. She took a step forward, as if to the first strain of some formal dance, and moved close, facing me. For an instant a grilled window had framed her head and shoulders and a rich tapestry had adorned the wall to her left. Planned and posed, of course. Still, effective. She held my Trump in her left hand. She smiled. The others glanced our way as she appeared and she hit them all with that smile, like the Mona Lisa with a machine gun, turning slowly.

"Corwin," she said, kissing me briefly and withdrawing, "I fear I am early."

"Never," I replied, turning toward Random, who had just risen and who anticipated me by seconds.

"May I fetch you a drink, sister?" he asked, taking her hand and nodding toward the sideboard.

"Why, yes. Thank you," and he led her off and poured her some wine, avoiding or at least postponing, I suppose, her usual clash with Flora. At least, I assumed most of the old frictions were still alive as I remembered them. So if it cost me her company for the moment it also maintained the domestic-tranquility index, which was important to me just then. Random can be good at such things when he wants to.

I drummed the side of the desk with my fingertips, I rubbed my aching shoulder, I uncrossed and re-crossed my legs, I debated lighting a cigarette. . . .

Suddenly he was there. At the far end of the room, Gérard had turned to his left, said something, and extended his hand. An instant later, he was clasping the left and only hand of Benedict, the final member of our group.

All right. The fact that Benedict had chosen to come in on Gérard's Trump rather than mine was his way of expressing his feelings toward me. Was it also an indication of an alliance to keep me in check? It was at least calculated to make me wonder. Could it have been Benedict who had put Gérard up to our morning's exercise? Probably.

At that moment Julian rose to his feet, crossed the room, gave Benedict a word and a handclasp. This activity attracted Llewella. She turned, closing her book and laying it aside. Smiling then, she advanced and greeted Benedict, nodded to Julian, said something to Gérard. The impromptu conference warmed, grew animated. All right again, and again.

Four and three. And two in the middle . . .

I waited, staring at the group across the room. We were all present, and I could have asked them for attention and proceeded with what I had in mind. However . . .

It was too tempting. All of us could feel the tension, I knew. It was as if a pair of magnetic poles had suddenly been activated within the room. I was curious to see how all the filings would fall.

Flora gave me one quick glance. I doubted that she had changed her mind overnight—unless, of course, there had been some new development. No, I felt confident that I had anticipated the next move.

Nor was I incorrect. I overheard her mentioning thirst and a glass of wine. She turned partway and made a move in my direction, as if expecting Fiona to accompany her. She hesitated for a moment when this did not occur, suddenly became the focus of the

entire company's attention, realized this fact, made a
quick decision, smiled, and moved in my direction.

"Corwin," she said, "I believe I would like a glass
of wine."

Without turning my head or removing my gaze from
the tableau before me, I called back over my shoulder,
"Random, pour Flora a glass of wine, would you?"

"But of course," he replied, and I heard the necessary sounds.

Flora nodded, unsmiled, and passed beyond me to
the right.

Four and four, leaving dear Fiona burning brightly
in the middle of the room. Totally self-conscious and
enjoying it, she immediately turned toward the oval
mirror with the dark, intricately carved frame, hanging
in the space between the two nearest tiers of shelves.
She proceeded to adjust a stray strand of hair in the
vicinity of her left temple.

Her movement produced a flash of green and silver
among the red and gold geometries of the carpet, near
to the place where her left foot had rested.

I had simultaneous desires to curse and to smile.
The arrant bitch was playing games with us again.
Always remarkable, though . . . Nothing had changed.
Neither cursing nor smiling, I moved forward, as she
had known I would.

But Julian too approached, and a trifle more quickly
than I. He had been a bit nearer, may have spotted it
a fraction of an instant sooner.

He scooped it up and dangled it gently.

"Your bracelet, sister," he said pleasantly. "It seems
to have forsaken your wrist, foolish thing. Here—allow
me."

She extended her hand, giving him one of those
lowered-eyelash smiles while he unfastened her chain
of emeralds. Completing the business, he folded her
hand within both of his own and began to turn back
toward his corner, from whence the others were cast-

ing sidelong glances while attempting to seem locally occupied.

"I believe you would be amused by a witticism we are about to share," he began.

Her smile grew even more delightful as she disengaged her hand.

"Thank you, Julian," she replied. "I am certain that when I hear it I will laugh. Last, as usual, I fear." She turned and took my arm. "I find that I feel a greater desire," she said, "for a glass of wine."

So I took her back with me and saw her refreshed. Five and four.

Julian, who dislikes showing strong feelings, reached a decision a few moments later and followed us over. He poured himself a glass, sipped from it, studied me for ten or fifteen seconds, then said, "I believe we are all present now. When do you plan to proceed with whatever you have in mind?"

"I see no reason for further delay," I said, "now that everyone has had his turn." I raised my voice then and directed it across the room. "The time has come. Let us get comfortable."

The others drifted over. Chairs were dragged up and settled into. More wine was poured. A minute later we had an audience.

"Thank you," I said when the final stirrings had subsided. "I have a number of things I would like to say, and some of them might even get said. The course of it all will depend on what goes before, and we will get into that right now. Random, tell them what you told me yesterday."

"All right."

I withdrew to the seat behind the desk and Random moved to occupy the edge of it. I leaned back and listened again to the story of his communication with Brand and his attempt to rescue him. It was a condensed version, bereft of the speculations which had not really strayed from my consciousness since Random had put them there. And despite their omission, a tacit awareness of the implications was occurring within all the others. I knew that. It was the main reason I had wanted Random to speak first. Had I simply come out with an attempt to make a case for my suspicions, I would almost certainly have been assumed to be engaged in the time-honored practice of directing attention away from myself—an act to be followed immediately by the separate, sharp, metallic clicks of minds snapping shut against me. This way, despite any thoughts that Random would say whatever I wanted him to say, they would hear him out, wondering the while. They would toy with the ideas, attempting to foresee the point of my having called the assembly in the first place. They would allow the time that would permit the premises to take root contingent upon later corroboration. And they would be wondering whether we could produce the evidence. I was wondering that same thing myself.

While I waited and wondered I watched the others, a fruitless yet inevitable exercise. Simple curiosity, more than suspicion even, required that I search these faces for reactions, clues, indications—the faces that I knew better than any others, to the limits of my understanding such things. And of course they told me nothing. Perhaps it is true that you really only look at a person the first time you see him, and after that you do a quick bit of mental shorthand each time you recognize him. My brain is lazy enough to give that its likelihood, using its abstracting powers and a presumption of regularity to avoid work whenever possible. This time I forced myself to see, though, and it still did not help. Julian maintained his slightly bored, slightly amused mask. Gérard appeared alternately surprised, angry, and wistful. Benedict just looked bleak and suspicious. Llewella seemed as sad and inscrutable as ever. Deirdre looked distracted, Flora acquiescent, and Fiona was studying everyone else, myself included, assembling her own catalog of reactions.

The only thing that I could tell, after some time,

was that Random was making an impression. While no one betrayed himself, I saw the boredom vanish, the old suspicion abate, the new suspicion come to life. Interest rose among my kin. Fascination, almost. Then everyone had questions. At first a few, then a barrage.

"Wait," I finally interrupted. "Let him finish. The whole thing. Some of these will answer themselves. Get the others afterward."

There were nods and growls, and Random proceeded through to the real end. That is, he carried it on to our fight with the beastmen at Flora's, indicating that they were of the same ilk as the one who had slain Caine. Flora endorsed this part.

Then, when the questions came, I watched them carefully. So long as they dealt with the matter of Random's story, they were all to the good. But I wanted to cut things short of speculation as to the possibility of one of us being behind it all. As soon as that came out, talk of me and the smell of red herrings would also drift in. This could lead to ugly words and the emergence of a mood I was not anxious to engender. Better to go for the proof first, save on later recriminations, corner the culprit right now if possible, and consolidate my position on the spot.

So I watched and waited. When I felt that the vital moment had ticked its way too near I stopped the clock.

"None of this discussion, this speculation, would be necessary," I said, "if we had all of the facts right now. And there may be a way to get them—right now. That is why you are here."

That did it. I had them. Attentive. Ready. Maybe even willing.

"I propose we attempt to reach Brand and bring him home," I said, "now."

"How?" Benedict asked me.

"The Trumps."

"It has been tried," said Julian. "He cannot be reached that way. No response."

"I was not referring to the ordinary usage," I said.

"I asked you all to bring full sets of Trumps with you. I trust that you have them?"

There were nods.

"Good," I said. "Let us shuffle out Brand's Trump now. I propose that all nine of us attempt to contact him simultaneously."

"An interesting thought," Benedict said.

"Yes," Julian agreed, producing his deck and riffling through it. "Worth trying, at least. It may generate additional power. I do not really know."

I located Brand's Trump. I waited until all the others had found it. Then, "Let us coordinate things," I said. "Is everyone ready?"

Eight assents were spoken.

"Then go ahead. Try. Now."

I studied my card. Brand's features were similar to my own, but he was shorter and slenderer. His hair was like Fiona's. He wore a green riding suit. He rode a white horse. How long ago? How long ago was that? I wondered. Something of a dreamer, a mystic, a poet, Brand was always disillusioned or elated, cynical or wholly trusting. His feelings never seemed to find a middle ground. Manic-depressive is too facile a term for his complex character, yet it might serve to indicate a direction of departure, multitudes of qualifications lining the roadway thereafter. Pursuant to this state of affairs, I must admit that there were times when I found him so charming, considerate, and loyal that I valued him above all my other kin. Other times, however, he could be so bitter, sarcastic, and downright savage that I tried to avoid his company for fear that I might do him harm. Summing up, the last time I had seen him had been one of the latter occasions, just a bit before Eric and I had had the falling out that led to my exile from Amber.

. . . And those were my thoughts and feelings as I studied his Trump, reaching out to him with my mind, my will, opening the vacant place I sought him to fill.

About me, the others shuffled their own memories and did the same.

Slowly the card took on a dream-dust quality and acquired the illusion of depth. There followed that familiar blurring, with the sense of movement which heralds contact with the subject. The Trump grew colder beneath my fingertips, and then things flowed and formed, achieving a sudden verity of vision, persistent, dramatic, full.

He seemed to be in a cell. There was a stone wall behind him. There was straw on the floor. He was manacled, and his chain ran back through a huge ring bolt set in the wall above and behind him. It was a fairly long chain, providing sufficient slack for movement, and at the moment he was taking advantage of this fact, lying sprawled on a heap of straw and rags off in the corner. His hair and beard were quite long, his face thinner than I had ever before seen it. His clothes were tattered and filthy. He seemed to be sleeping. My mind went back to my own imprisonment— the smells, the cold, the wretched fare, the dampness, the loneliness, the madness that came and went. At least he still had his eyes, for they flickered and I saw them when several of us spoke his name; green they were, with a flat, vacant look.

Was he drugged? Or did he believe himself to be hallucinating?

But suddenly his spirit returned. He raised himself. He extended his hand.

"Brothers!" he said. "Sisters . . ."

"I'm coming!" came a shout that shook the room.

Gérard had leaped to his feet, knocking over his chair. He dashed across the room and snatched a great battle ax from its pegs on the wall. He slung it at his wrist, holding the Trump in that same hand. For a moment he froze, studying the card. Then he extended his free hand and suddenly he was there, clasping Brand, who chose that moment to pass out again. The image wavered. The contact was broken.

Cursing, I sought through the pack after Gérard's own Trump. Several of the others seemed to be doing the same thing. Locating it, I moved for contact. Slowly, the melting, the turning, the re-forming occurred. There!

Gérard had drawn the chain taut across the stones of the wall and was attacking it with the ax. It was a heavy thing, however, and resisted his powerful blows for a long while. Eventually several of the links were mashed and scarred, but by then he had been at it for almost two minutes, and the ringing, chopping sounds had alerted the jailers.

For there were noises from the left—a rattling sound, the sliding of bolts, the creaking of hinges. Although my field of perception did not extend that far, it seemed obvious that the cell's door was being opened. Brand raised himself once more. Gérard continued to hack at the chain.

"Gérard! The door!" I shouted.

"I know!" he bellowed, wrapping the chain about his arm and yanking it. It did not yield.

Then he let go of the chain and swung the ax, as one of the horny-handed warriors rushed him, blade upraised. The swordsman fell, to be replaced by another. Then a third and a fourth crowded by them. Others were close on their heels.

There was a blur of movement at that moment and Random knelt within the tableau, his right hand clasped with Brand's, his left holding his chair before him like a shield, its legs pointing outward. He sprang to his feet and rushed the attackers, driving the chair like a battering ram amid them. They fell back. He raised the chair and swung it. One lay dead on the floor, felled by Gérard's ax. Another had drawn off to one side, clutching at the stump of his right arm. Random produced a dagger and left it in a nearby stomach, brained two more with the chair, and drove back the final man. Eerily, while this was going on, the dead man rose above the floor and slowly drifted upward, spilling and dripping the while. The one who had been stabbed collapsed to his knees, clutching at the blade.

In the meantime, Gérard had taken hold of the chain with both hands. He braced one foot against the wall and commenced to pull. His shoulders rose as the great muscles tightened across his back. The chain held. Ten seconds, perhaps. Fifteen . . .

Then, with a snap and a rattle, it parted. Gérard stumbled backward, catching himself with an outflung hand. He glanced back, apparently at Random, who was out of my line of sight at the moment. Seemingly satisfied, he turned away, stooped and raised Brand, who had fallen unconscious again. Holding him in his arms, he turned and extended one hand from beneath the limp form. Random leaped back into sight beside them, *sans* chair, and gestured to us also.

All of us reached for them, and a moment later they stood amid us and we crowded around.

A sort of cheer had gone up as we rushed to touch him, to see him, our brother who had been gone these many years and just now snatched back from his mysterious captors. And at last, hopefully, finally, some answers might also have been liberated. Only he looked so weak, so thin, so pale. . . .

"Get back!" Gérard shouted. "I'm taking him to the couch! Then you can look all you—"

Dead silence. For everyone had backed off, and then turned to stone. This was because there was blood on Brand, and it was dripping. And this was because there was a knife in his left side, to the rear. It had not been there moments before. Some one of us had just tried for his kidney and possibly succeeded. I was not heartened by the fact that the Random-Corwin Conjecture that it was One Of Us Behind It All had just received a significant boost. I had an instant during which to concentrate all my faculties in an attempt to mentally photograph everyone's position. Then the spell was broken. Gérard bore Brand to the couch and we drew aside; and we all knew that we all realized not only what had happened, but what it implied.

Gérard set Brand down in a prone position and tore away his filthy shirt.

"Get me clean water to bathe him," he said. "And towels. Get me saline solution and glucose and something to hang them from. Get me a whole medical kit."

Deirdre and Flora moved toward the door.

"My quarters are closest," said Random. "One of you will find a medical kit there. But the only IV stuff is in the lab on the third floor. I'd better come and help."

They departed together.

We all had had medical training somewhere along the line, both here and abroad. That which we learned in Shadow, though, had to be modified in Amber. Most antibiotics from the shadow worlds, for example, were ineffectual here. On the other hand, our personal immunological processes appear to behave differently from those of any other peoples we have studied, so that it is much more difficult for us to become infected —and if infected we deal with it more expeditiously. Then, too, we possess profound regenerative abilities.

All of which is as it must be, of course, the ideal necessarily being superior to its shadows. And Amberites that we are, and aware of these facts from an early age, all of us obtained medical training relatively early in life. Basically, despite what is often said about being your own physician, it goes back to our not unjustified distrust of virtually everyone, and most particularly of those who might hold our lives in their hands. All of which partly explains why I did not rush to shoulder Gérard aside to undertake Brand's treatment myself, despite the fact that I had been through a med school on the shadow Earth within the past couple of generations. The other part of the explanation is that Gérard was not letting anyone else near Brand. Julian and Fiona had both moved forward, apparently with the same thing in mind, only to encounter Gérard's left arm like a gate at a railway crossing.

"No," he had said. "I know that I did not do it, and that is all that I know. There will be no second chance for anyone else."

With any one of us sustaining that sort of wound while in an otherwise sound condition, I would say that if he made it through the first half hour he would make it. Brand, though . . . The shape he was in . . . There was no telling.

When the others returned with the materials and equipment, Gérard cleaned Brand, sutured the wound, and dressed it. He hooked up the IV, broke off the manacles with a hammer and chisel Random had located, covered Brand with a sheet and a blanket, and took his pulse again.

"How is it?" I asked.

"Weak," he said, and he drew up a chair and seated himself beside the couch. "Someone fetch me my blade —and a glass of wine. I didn't have any. Also, if there is any food left over there, I'm hungry."

Llewella headed for the sideboard and Random got him his blade from the rack behind the door.

"Are you just going to camp there?" Random asked, passing him the weapon.

"I am."

"What about moving Brand to a better bed?"

"He is all right where he is. I will decide when he can be moved. In the meantime, someone get a fire going. Then put out a few of those candles."

Random nodded.

"I'll do it," he said. Then he picked up the knife Gérard had drawn from Brand's side, a thin stiletto, its blade about seven inches in length. He held it across the palm of his hand.

"Does anyone recognize this?" he asked.

"Not I," said Benedict.

"Nor I," said Julian.

"No," I said.

The girls shook their heads.

Random studied it.

"Easily concealed—up a sleeve, in a boot or bodice. It took real nerve to use it that way. . . ."

"Desperation," I said.

". . . And a very accurate anticipation of our mob scene. Inspired, almost."

"Could one of the guards have done it?" Julian asked. "Back in the cell?"

"No," Gérard said. "None of them came near enough."

"It looks to be decently balanced for throwing," Deirdre said.

"It is," said Random, shifting it about his fingertips. "Only none of them had a clear shot or the opportunity. I'm positive.

Llewella returned, bearing a tray containing slabs of meat, half a loaf of bread, a bottle of wine, and a goblet. I cleared a small table and set it beside Gérard's chair. As Llewella deposited the tray, she asked, "But why? That only leaves us. Why would one of us want to do it?"

I sighed.

"Whose prisoner do you think he might have been?" I asked.

"One of us?"

"If he possessed knowledge which someone was willing to go to this length to suppress, what do you think? The same reason also served to put him where he was and keep him there."

Her brows tightened.

"That does not make sense either. Why didn't they just kill him and be done with it?"

I shrugged.

"Must have had some use for him," I said. "But there is really only one person who can answer that question adequately. When you find him, ask him."

"Or her," Julian said. "Sister, you seem possessed of a superabundance of naïveté, suddenly."

Her gaze locked with Julian's own, a pair of icebergs reflecting frigid infinities.

"As I recall," she said, "you rose from your seat when they came through, turned to the left, rounded the desk, and stood slightly to Gérard's right. You leaned pretty far forward. I believe your hands were out of sight, below."

"And as I recall," he said, "you were within striking distance yourself, off to Gérard's left—and leaning forward."

"I would have had to do it with my left hand—and I am right-handed."

"Perhaps he owes what life he still possesses to that fact."

"You seem awfully anxious, Julian, to find that it was someone else."

"All right," I said. "All right! You know this is self-defeating. Only one of us did it, and this is not the way to smoke him out."

"Or her," Julian added.

Gérard rose, towered, glared.

"I will not have you disturbing my patient," he said. "And, Random, you said you were going to see to the fire."

"Right away," Random said, and moved to do it.

"Let us adjourn to the sitting room off the main hall," I said, "downstairs. Gérard, I will post a couple of guards outside the door here."

"No," Gérard said. "I would rather that anyone who wishes to try it get this far. I will hand you his head in the morning."

I nodded.

"Well, you can ring for anything you need—or call one of us on the Trumps. We will fill you in in the morning on anything that we learn."

Gérard seated himself, grunted, and began eating. Random got the fire going and extinguished some lights.

Brand's blanket rose and fell, slowly but regularly. We filed quietly from the room and headed for the stairway, leaving them there together with the flare and the crackle, the tubes and the bottles.

7

Many are the times I have awakened, sometimes shaking, always afraid, from the dream that I occupied my old cell, blind once more, in the dungeons beneath Amber. It is not as if I were unfamiliar with the condition of imprisonment. I have been locked away on a number of occasions, for various periods of time. But solitary, plus blindness with small hope of recovery, made for a big charge at the sensory-deprivation counter in the department store of the mind. That, with the sense of finality to it all, had left its marks. I generally keep these memories safely tucked away during waking hours, but at night, sometimes, they come loose, dance down the aisles and frolic round the notions counter, one, two, three. Seeing Brand there in his cell had brought them out again, along with an unseasonal chill; and that final thrust served to establish a more or less permanent residence for them. Now, among my kin in the shield-hung sitting room, I could not avoid the thought that one or more of them had done unto Brand as Eric had done unto me. While this capacity was in itself hardly a surprising discovery, the matter of occupying the same room with the culprit and having no idea as to his identity was more than a little disturbing. My only consolation was that each of the others, according to his means, must be disturbed also. Including the guilty, now that the existence theorem had shown a positive. I knew then that I had been hoping all along that outsiders were entirely to blame. Now, though . . . On the one hand I felt even more restricted

than usual in what I could say. On the other, it seemed
a good time to press for information, with everyone in
an abnormal state of mind. The desire to cooperate for
purposes of dealing with the threat could prove help-
ful. And even the guilty party would want to behave
the same as everyone else. Who knew but that he
might slip up while making the effort?

"Well, have you any other interesting little experiments you would care to conduct?" Julian asked me,
clasping his hands behind his head and leaning back
in my favorite chair.

"Not at the moment," I said.

"Pity," he replied. "I was hoping you would suggest
we go looking for Dad now in the same fashion. Then,
if we are lucky, we find him and someone puts him out
of the way with more certainty. After that, we could
all play Russian roulette with those fine new weapons
you've furnished—winner take all."

"Your words are ill-considered," I said.

"Not so. I considered every one of them," he answered. "We spend so much time lying to one another
that I decided it might be amusing to say what I really
felt. Just to see whether anyone noticed."

"Now you see that we have. We also notice that the
real you is no improvement over the old one."

"Whichever you prefer, both of us have been wondering whether you have any idea what you are going
to do next."

"I do," I said. "I now intend to obtain answers to a
number of questions dealing with everything that is
plaguing us. We might as well start with Brand and his
troubles." Turning toward Benedict, who was sitting
gazing into the fire, I said, "Back in Avalon, Benedict,
you told me that Brand was one of the ones who
searched for me after my disappearance."

"That is correct," Benedict answered.

"All of us went looking," Julian said.

"Not at first," I replied. "Initially, it was Brand,

Gérard, and yourself, Benedict. Isn't that what you told me?"

"Yes," he said. "The others did have a go at it later, though. I told you that, too."

I nodded.

"Did Brand report anything unusual at that time?" I asked.

"Unusual? In what way?" said Benedict.

"I don't know. I am looking for some connection between what happened to him and what happened to me."

"Then you are looking in the wrong place," Benedict said. "He returned and reported no success. And he was around for ages after that, unmolested."

"I gathered that much," I said. "I understand from what Random has told me, though, that his final disappearance occurred approximately a month before my own recovery and return. That almost strikes me as peculiar. If he did not report anything special after his return from the search, did he do so prior to his disappearance? Or in the interim? Anyone? Anything? Say it if you've got it!"

There followed some mutual glancing about. The looks seemed more curious than suspicious or nervous, though.

Finally, then, "Well," Llewella said, "I do not know. Do not know whether it is significant, I mean."

All eyes came to rest upon her. She began to knot and unknot the ends of her belt cord, slowly, as she spoke.

"It was in the interim, and it may have no bearing," she went on. "It is just something that struck me as peculiar. Brand came to Rebma long ago—"

"How long ago?" I asked.

She furrowed her brow.

"Fifty, sixty, seventy years . . . I am not certain."

I tried to summon up the rough conversion factor I had worked out during my long incarceration. A day in Amber, it seemed, constituted a bit over two and a half days on the shadow Earth where I had spent my exile. I wanted to relate events in Amber to my own time-scale whenever possible, just in case any peculiar correspondences turned up. So Brand had gone to Rebma sometime in what was, to me, the nineteenth century.

"Whatever the date," she said, "he came and visited me. Stayed for several weeks." She glanced at Random then. "He was asking about Martin."

Random narrowed his eyes and cocked his head.

"Did he say why?" he asked her.

"Not exactly," she said. "He implied that he had met Martin somewhere in his travels, and he gave the impression that he would like to get in touch with him again. I did not realize until some time after his departure that finding out everything he could concerning Martin was probably the entire reason for his visit. You know how subtle Brand can be, finding out things without seeming to be after them. It was only after I had spoken with a number of others whom he had visited that I began to see what had occurred. I never did find out why, though."

"That is—most peculiar," Random observed. "For it brings to mind something to which I had never attached any significance. He once questioned me at great length concerning my son—and it may well have been at about the same time. He never indicated that he had met him, however—or that he had any desire to do so. It started out as a bit of banter on the subject of bastards. When I took offense he apologized and asked a number of more proper questions about the boy, which I assumed he then put for the sake of politeness —to leave me with a softer remembrance. As you say, though, he had a way of drawing admissions from people. Why is it you never told me of this before?"

She smiled prettily.

"Why should I have?" she said.

Random nodded slowly, his face expressionless.

"Well, what did you tell him?" he said. "What did

he learn? What do you know about Martin that I don't?"

She shook her head, her smile fading.

"Nothing—actually," she said. "To my knowledge, no one in Rebma ever heard from Martin after he took the Pattern and vanished. I do not believe that Brand departed knowing any more than he did when he arrived."

"Strange . . ." I said. "Did he approach anyone else on the subject?"

"I don't remember," Julian said.

"Nor I," said Benedict.

The others shook their heads.

"Then let us note it and leave it for now," I said. "There are other things I also need to know. Julian, I understand that you and Gérard attempted to follow the black road a while back, and that Gérard was injured along the way. I believe you both stayed with Benedict for a time after that, while Gérard recuperated. I would like to know about that expedition."

"It seems as if you already do," Julian replied. "You have just stated everything that occurred."

"Where did you learn of this, Corwin," Benedict inquired.

"Back in Avalon," I said.

"From whom?"

"Dara," I said.

He rose to his feet, came over, stood before me, glared down.

"You still persist in that absurd story about the girl!"

I sighed.

"We have been round and round on this too many times," I said. "By now I have told you everything that I know on the subject. Either you accept it or you do not. She is the one who told me, though."

"Apparently, then, there were some things you did not tell me. You never mentioned that part before."

"Is it true or isn't it? About Julian and Gérard."

"It is true," he said.

"Then forget the source for now and let us get on with what happened."

"Agreed," Benedict said. "I may speak candidly, now that the reason for secrecy is no longer with us. Eric, of course. He was unaware of my whereabouts, as were most of the others. Gérard was my main source of news in Amber. Eric grew more and more apprehensive concerning the black road and finally decided to send scouts to trace it through Shadow to its source. Julian and Gérard were selected. They were attacked by a very strong party of its creatures at a point near Avalon. Gérard called to me, via my Trump, for assistance and I went to their aid. The enemy was dispatched. As Gérard had sustained a broken leg in the fighting and Julian was a bit battered himself, I took them both home with me. I broke my silence with Eric at that time, to tell him where they were and what had become of them. He ordered them not to continue their journey, but to return to Amber after they had recovered. They remained with me until they did. Then they went back."

"That is all?"

"That is all."

But it wasn't. Dara had also told me something else. She had mentioned another visitor. I remembered it quite distinctly. That day, beside the stream, a tiny rainbow in the mist above the waterfall, the mill wheel turning round and round, delivering dreams and grinding them, that day we had fenced and talked and walked in Shadow, had passed through a primordial wood, coming to a spot beside a mighty torrent where turned a wheel fit for the granary of the gods, that day we had picnicked, flirted, gossiped, she had told me many things, some of them doubtless false. But she had not lied concerning the journey of Julian and Gérard, and I believed it possible that she had also spoken truly when she said that Brand had visited Benedict in Avalon. "Frequently" was the word she had used.

Now, Benedict made no secret of the fact that he distrusted me. I could see this alone as sufficient reason for his withholding information on anything he judged too sensitive to become my business. Hell, buying his story, I would not have trusted me either if our situations were reversed. Only a fool would have called him on it at that moment, though. Because of the other possibilities.

It could be that he planned to tell me later, in private, of the circumstances surrounding Brand's visits. They could well have involved something he did not wish to discuss before the group, and especially before Brand's would-be killer.

Or— There was, of course, the possibility that Benedict himself was behind it all. I did not even like to think about the consequences. Having served under Napoleon, Lee, and MacArthur, I appreciated the tactician as well as the strategist. Benedict was both, and he was the best I had ever known. The recent loss of his right arm had in no way diminished him in this, or for that matter impaired his personal fighting skills. Had I not been very lucky recently he could easily have turned me into a pile of scallops over our misunderstanding. No, I did not want it to be Benedict, and I was not about to grope after whatever he had at that moment seen fit to conceal. I only hoped that he was just saving it for later.

So I settled for his, "That is all," and decided to move on to other matters.

"Flora," I said, "back when I first visited you, after my accident, you said something which I still do not quite understand. In that I had ample time relatively soon thereafter in which to review many things, I came across it in my memories and occasionally puzzled over it. I still do not understand it. So would you please tell me what you meant when you said that the shadows contained more horrors than any had thought?"

"Why, I do not properly recall saying it," Flora said. "But I suppose that I must have, if it made such an impression. You know the effect that I was referring to: that Amber seems to act as something of a magnet on adjacent shadows, drawing things across from them; the nearer you get to Amber the easier the road becomes, even for shadow-things. While there always seems to be some exchange of materials among adjacent shadows themselves, the effect is more forceful and also more of a one-way process when it comes to Amber. We have always been alert for peculiar things slipping through. Well, for several years prior to your recovery, more such things than usual seemed to be showing up in the vicinity of Amber. Dangerous things, almost invariably. Many were recognizable creatures from nearby realms. After a time, though, things kept coming in from farther and farther afield. Eventually, some which were totally unknown made it through. No reason could be found for this sudden transportation of menaces, although we sought fairly far for disturbances which might be driving them this way. In other words, highly improbable penetrations of Shadow were occurring."

"This actually began while Dad was still around?"

"Oh yes. It started several years before your recovery—as I said."

"I see. Did anyone consider the possibility of there being a connection between this state of affairs and Dad's departure?"

"Certainly," Benedict replied. "I still feel that that was the reason for it. He went off to investigate, or to seek a remedy."

"But that is purely conjecture," Julian said. "You know how he was. He gave no reasons."

Benedict shrugged.

"It is a reasonable inference, though," he said. "I understand that he had spoken of his concern over the —monster migrations, if you like—on numerous occasions."

I withdrew my cards from their case, having recently gotten into the habit of carrying a set of Trumps with me at all times. I raised Gérard's Trump and regarded it. The others were silent, watching me as I did this. Moments later, there was contact.

Gérard was still seated in his chair, his blade across his knees. He was still eating. He swallowed when he felt my presence and said, "Yes, Corwin? What do you want?"

"How is Brand?"

"Sleeping," he said. "His pulse is a little stronger. His breathing is the same—regular. It's still too early—"

"I know,"I said. "I mainly wanted to check your recollection of something: Near the end there, did you get the impression from anything he might have said or done that Dad's going away might have been connected with the increased number of Shadow beings that were slipping through into Amber?"

"That," said Julian, "is what is known as a leading question."

Gérard wiped his mouth.

"There could have been a connection, yes," he said. "He seemed disturbed, preoccupied with something. And he did talk about the creatures. But he never really said that that was his main concern—or whether it was something entirely different."

"Like what?"

He shook his head.

"Anything. I—yes . . . yes, there is something you probably ought to know, for whatever it is worth. Some time after his disappearance, I did make an effort to find out one thing. That was, whether I was indeed the last person to see him before his departure. I am fairly certain that I was. I had been here in the palace all evening, and I was preparing to return to the flagship. Dad had retired about an hour earlier, but I had stayed on in the guard room, playing draughts with Captain Thoben. As we were sailing the following morning, I decided to take a book with me. So I came up here to the library. Dad was seated at the desk." He gestured with his head. "He was going through some old books, and he had not yet changed his garments.

He nodded to me when I entered, and I told him I had just come up for a book. He said, 'You've come to the right place,' and he kept on reading. While I was looking over the shelves, he said something to the effect that he could not sleep. I found a book, told him good night, he said, 'Good sailing,' and I left." He lowered his eyes again. "Now I am positive he was wearing the Jewel of Judgment that night, that I saw it on him then as plainly as I see it on you now. I am equally certain that he had not had it on earlier that evening. For a long while after, I thought that he had taken it along with him, wherever he went. There was no indication in his chambers that he had later changed his clothing. I never saw the stone again until you and Bleys were defeated in your assault on Amber. Then, Eric was wearing it. When I questioned him he claimed that he had found it in Dad's chambers. Lacking evidence to the contrary, I had to accept his story. But I was never happy with it. Your question—and seeing you wearing it—has brought it all back. So I thought you had better know about it."

"Thanks," I said, and another question occurred to me but I decided against asking it at that moment. For the benefit of the others, I closed off by saying, "So do you think he needs any more blankets? Or anything else?"

Gérard raised his glass to me, then took a drink.

"Very good. Keep up the good work," I said, and I passed my hand over his card.

"Brother Brand seems to be doing all right," I said, "and Gérard does not recollect Dad's saying anything that would directly connect Shadow slippage and his departure. I wonder how Brand will recall things, when he comes around?"

"*If* he comes around," Julian said.

"I think that he will," I said. "We have all taken some pretty bad beatings. Our vitality is one of the few things we have come to trust. My guess is that he will be talking by morning."

"What do you propose doing with the guilty party," he asked, "if Brand names him?"

"Question him," I said.

"Then I would like to do the questioning. I am beginning to feel that you may be right this time, Corwin, and that the person who stabbed him may also be responsible for our intermittent state of siege, for Dad's disappearance, and for Caine's killing. So I would enjoy questioning him before we cut his throat, and I would like to volunteer for that last part also."

"We will keep it in mind," I said.

"You are not excluded from the reckoning, Corwin."

"I was aware of that."

"I have something to say," said Benedict, smothering a rejoinder from Julian. "I find myself troubled both by the strength and the apparent objective of the opposition. I have encountered them now on several occasions, and they *are* out for blood. Accepting for the moment your story of the girl Dara, Corwin, her final words do seem to sum up their attitude: 'Amber will be destroyed.' Not conquered, subjugated, or taught a lesson. Destroyed. Julian, you wouldn't mind ruling here, would you?"

Julian smiled.

"Perhaps next year this time," he said. "Not today, thank you."

"What I am getting at is that I could see you—or any of us—employing mercenaries or obtaining allies to effect a takeover. I cannot see you employing a force so powerful that it would represent a grave problem itself afterward. Not a force that seems bent on destruction rather than conquest. I cannot see you, me, Corwin, the others as actually trying to destroy Amber, or willing to gamble with forces that would. That is the part I do not like about Corwin's notion that one of us is behind this."

I had to nod. I was not unaware of the weakness of that link in my chain of speculations. Still, there were so many unknowns. . . . I could offer alternatives, such as Random then did, but guesses prove nothing.

"It may be," Random said, "that one of us made the deal but underestimated his allies. The guilty party may now be sweating this thing as much as the rest of us. He may not be in a position to turn things off now, even if he wants to."

"We could offer him the opportunity," Fiona said, "to betray his allies to us now. If Julian could be persuaded to leave his throat uncut and the rest of us were willing to do the same, he might come around— if Random's guess is correct. He would not claim the throne, but he was obviously not about to have it before. He would have his life and he could save Amber quite a bit of trouble. Is anyone willing to commit himselm to a position on this?"

"I am," I said. "I will give him life if he will come across, with the understanding that it will be spent in exile."

"I will go along with that," Benedict said.

"So will I," said Random.

"On one condition," Julian said. "If he was not personally responsible for Caine's death, I will go along with it. Otherwise, no. And there would have to be evidence."

"Life, in exile," Deirdre said. "All right. I agree."

"So do I," said Flora.

"And I," Llewella followed.

"Gérard will probably agree too," I said. "But I really wonder whether Brand will feel the same as the rest of us. I've a feeling he may not."

"Let us check with Gérard," Benedict said. "If Brand makes it and proves the only holdout, the guilty party will know he has only one enemy to avoid—and they can always work out their own terms on that count."

"All right," I said, smothering a few misgivings, and I recontacted Gérard, who agreed also.

So we rose to our feet and swore that much by the

Unicorn of Amber—Julian's oath having an extra
clause to it—and swore to enforce exile on any of our
own number who violated the oath. Frankly, I did not
think it would net us anything, but it is always nice to
see families doing things together.

After that, everyone made a point of mentioning that
he would be remaining in the palace overnight, presumably to indicate that no one feared anything Brand
might have to say in the morning—and especially to
indicate that no one had a desire to get out of town,
a thing that would not be forgotten, even if Brand gave
up the ghost during the night. In that I had no further
questions to put to the group and no one had sprung
forward to own up to the misdeeds covered by the
oath, I leaned back and listened for a time after that.
Things came apart, falling into a series of conversa-
tions and exchanges, one of the main topics being an
attempted reconstruction of the library tableau, each
of us in his own place and, invariably, why each of us
was in a position to have done it, except for the speaker.
I smoked; I said nothing on the subject. Deirdre did
spot an interesting possibility, however. Namely, that
Gérard could have done the stabbing himself while we
were all crowded around, and that his heroic efforts
were not prompted by any desire to save Brand's neck,
but rather to achieve a position where he could stop
his tongue—in which case Brand would never make
it through the night. Ingenious, but I just couldn't believe it. No one else bought it either. At least, no one
volunteered to go upstairs and throw Gérard out.

After a time Fiona drifted over and sat beside me.

"Well, I've tried the only thing I could think of," she
said. "I hope some good comes of it."

"It may," I said.

"I see that you have added a peculiar piece of orna-
mentation to your wardrobe," she said, raising the
Jewel of Judgment between her thumb and forefinger
and studying it.

Then she raised her eyes.

"Can you make it do tricks for you?" she asked.

"Some," I said.

"Then you knew how to attune it. It involves the Pattern, doesn't it?"

"Yes. Eric told me how to go about it, right before he died."

"I see."

She released it, settled back into her seat, regarded the flames.

"Did he give you any cautions to go along with it?" she asked.

"No," I said.

"I wonder whether that was a matter of design or circumstance?"

"Well, he was pretty busy dying at the time. That limited our conversation considerably."

"I know. I was wondering whether his hatred for you outweighed his hopes for the realm, or whether he was simply ignorant of some of the principles involved."

"What do you know about it?"

"Think again of Eric's death, Corwin. I was not there when it occurred, but I came in early for the funeral. I was present when his body was bathed, shaved, dressed—and I examined his wounds. I do not believe that any of them were fatal, in themselves. There were three chest wounds, but only one looked as if it might have run into the mediastinal area—"

"One's enough, if—"

"Wait," she said. "It was difficult, but I tried judging the angle of the puncture with a thin glass rod. I wanted to make an incision, but Caine would not permit it. Still, I do not believe that his heart or arteries were damaged. It is still not too late to order an autopsy, if you would like me to check further on this. I am certain that his injuries and the general stress contributed to his death, but I believe it was the jewel that made the difference."

"Why do you think this?"

"Because of some things that Dworkin said when I

studied with him—and things that I noticed afterward, because of this. He indicated that while it con-
ferred unusual abilities, it also represented a drain
on the vitality of its master. The longer you wear it,
the more it somehow takes out of you. I paid attention after that, and I noticed that Dad wore it only
seldom and never kept it on for long periods of time."

My thoughts returned to Eric, the day he lay dying
on the slopes of Kolvir, the battle raging about him.
I remembered my first look at him, his face pale, his
breath labored, blood on his chest. . . . And the Jewel
of Judgment, there on its chain, was pulsing, heartlike,
among the moist folds of his garments. I had never
seen it do that before, or since. I recalled that the effect
had grown fainter, weaker. And when he died and I
folded his hands atop it, the phenomenon had ceased.

"What do you know of its function?" I asked her.

She shook her head.

"Dworkin considered that a state secret. I know the
obvious—weather control—and I inferred from some
of Dad's remarks that it has something to do with a
heightened perception, or a higher perception. Dworkin
had mentioned it primarily as an example of the per-
vasiveness of the Pattern in everything that gives us
power—even the Trumps contain the Pattern, if you
look closely, look long enough—and he cited it as an
instance of a conservation principle: all of our special
powers have their price. The greater the power, the
larger the investment. The Trumps are a small matter,
but there is still an element of fatigue involved in their
employment. Walking through Shadow, which is an
exercise of the image of the Pattern which exists within
us, is an even greater expenditure. To essay the Pattern
itself, physically, is a massive drain on one's energies.
But the jewel, he said, represents an even higher octave of the same thing, and its cost to its employer is
exponentially greater."

Thus, if correct, another ambiguous insight into the
character of my late and least favored brother. If he

were aware of this phenomenon and had donned the jewel and worn it overlong anyhow, in the defense of Amber, it made him something of a hero. But then, seen in this light, his passing it along to me, without warnings, became a deathbed effort at a final piece of vengeance. But he had exempted me from his curse, he'd said, so as to spend it properly on our enemies in the field. This, of course, only meant that he hated them a little more than he hated me and was deploying his final energies as strategically as possible, for Amber. I thought then of the partial character of Dworkin's notes, as I had recovered them from the hiding place Eric had indicated. Could it be that Eric had acquired them intact and had purposely destroyed that portion containing the cautions so as to damn his successor? That notion did not strike me as quite adequate, for he had had no way of knowing that I would return when I did, as I did, that the course of battle would run as it had, and that I would indeed be his successor. It could just as easily have been one of his favorites that followed him to power, in which case he would certainly not have wanted him to inherit any booby traps. No. As I saw it, either Eric was not really aware of this property of the stone, having acquired only partial instructions for its use, or someone had gotten to those papers before I had and removed sufficient material to leave me with a mortal liability. It may well have been the hand of the real enemy, once again.

"Do you know the safety factor?" I asked.

"No," she said. "I can give you only two pointers, for whatever they may be worth. The first is that I do not recall Dad's ever wearing it for long periods of time. The second, I pieced together from a number of things that he said, beginning with a comment to the effect that 'when people turn into statues you are either in the wrong place or in trouble.' I pressed him quite a bit on that, over a long period of time, and I eventually got the impression that the first sign of having worn it too long is some sort of distortion of your time sense.

Apparently it begins speeding up the metabolism—every-thing—with a net effect that the world seems to be slowing down around you. This must take quite a toll on a person. That is everything that I know about it, and I admit that a large part of the last is guesswork. How long have you been wearing it?"

"A while now," I said, taking my mental pulse and glancing about to see whether things seemed to be slow-ing down any.

I could not really tell, though of course I did not feel in the best of shape. I had assumed it was totally Gérard's doing, though. I was not about to yank it off, however, just because another family member had sug-gested it, even if it was clever Fiona in one of her friendlier moods. Perversity, cussedness . . . No, inde-pendence. That was it. That and purely formal distrust. I had only put it on for the evening a few hours before, anyway. I'd wait.

"Well, you have made your point in wearing it," she was saying. "I simply wanted to advise you against pro-longed exposure until you know more about it.

"Thanks, Fi. I'll have it off soon, and I appreciate your telling me. By the way, whatever became of Dworkin?"

She tapped her temple.

"His mind finally went, poor man. I like to think that Dad had him put away in some restful retreat in Shadow."

"I see what you mean," I said. "Yes, let us think that. Poor fellow."

Julian rose to his feet, concluding a conversation with Llewella. He stretched, nodded to her, and strolled over.

"Corwin, have you thought of any more questions for us?" he said.

"None that I'd care to ask just now."

He smiled.

"Anything more that you want to tell us?"

"Not at the moment."

"Any more experiments, demonstrations, charades?"

"No."

"Good. Then I'm going to bed. Good night."

"Night."

He bowed to Fiona, waved to Benedict and Random, nodded to Flora and Deirdre as he passed them on the way to the door. He paused on the threshold, turned back and said, "Now you can all talk about me," and went on out.

"All right," Fiona said. "Let's. I think he's the one."

"Why?" I asked.

"I'll go down the list, subjective, intuitive, and biased as it is. Benedict, in my opinion, is above suspicion. If he wanted the throne, he'd have it by now, by direct, military methods. With all the time he has had, he could have managed an attack that would have succeeded, even against Dad. He is that good, and we all know it. You, on the other hand, have made a number of blunders which you would not have made had you been in full possession of your faculties. That is why I believe your story, amnesia and all. No one gets himself blinded as a piece of strategy. Gérard is well on the way to establishing his own innocence. I almost think he is up there with Brand now more for that reason than from any desire to protect Brand. At any rate, we will know for sure before long—or else have some new suspicions. Random has simply been watched too closely these past years to have had the opportunity to engineer everything that has been happening. So he is out. Of us more delicate sorts, Flora hasn't the brains, Deirdre lacks the guts, Llewella hasn't the motivations, as she is happy elsewhere but never here, and I, of course, am innocent of all but malice. That leaves Julian. Is he capable? Yes. Does he want the throne? Of course. Has he had time and opportunity? Again, yes. He is your man."

"Would he have killed Caine?" I asked. "They were buddies."

She curled her lip.

"Julian has no friends," she said. "That icy personality of his is thawed only by thoughts of himself. Oh, in recent years he *seemed* closer to Caine than to anyone else. But even that . . . even that could have been a part of it. Shamming a friendship long enough to make it seem believable, so that he would not be suspect at this time. I can believe Julian capable of that because I cannot believe him capable of strong emotional attachments."

I shook my head.

"I don't know," I said. "His friendship with Caine is something that occurred during my absence, so everything I know concerning it is secondhand. Still, if Julian were looking for friendship in the form of another personality close to his own, I can see it. They were a lot alike. I tend to think it was real, because I don't think anybody is capable of deceiving someone about his friendship for years. Unless the other party is awfully stupid, which is something Caine was not. And— well, you say your reasoning was subjective, intuitive, and biased. So is mine, on something like this. I just don't like to think anybody is such a miserable wretch that he would use his only friend that way. That's why I think there is something wrong with your list."

She sighed.

"For someone who has been around for as long as you have, Corwin, you say some silly things. Were you changed by your long stay in that funny little place? Years ago you would have seen the obvious, as I do."

"Perhaps I have changed, for such things no longer seem obvious. Or could it be that you have changed, Fiona? A trifle more cynical than the little girl I once knew. It might not have been all that obvious to you, years ago."

She smiled softly.

"Never tell a woman she has changed, Corwin. Except for the better. You used to know that, too. Could it be that you are really only one of Corwin's shadows, sent back to suffer and intimidate here on his behalf? Is the real Corwin somewhere else, laughing at us all?"

"I am here, and I am not laughing," I said.

She laughed.

"Yes, that is it!" she said. "I have just decided that you are not yourself!

"Announcement, everybody!" she cried, springing to her feet. "I have just noticed that this is not really Corwin! It has to be one of his shadows! It has just announced a belief in friendship, dignity, nobility of spirit, and those other things which figure prominently in popular romances! I am obviously onto something!"

The others stared at her. She laughed again, then sat down abruptly.

I heard Flora mutter "drunk" and return to her conversation with Deirdre. Random said, "Let's hear it for shadows," and turned back to a discussion with Benedict and Llewella.

"See?" she said.

"What?"

"You're insubstantial," she said, patting my knee. "And so am I, now that I think about it. It has been a bad day, Corwin."

"I know. I feel like hell, too. I thought I had such a fine idea for getting Brand back. Not only that, it worked. A lot of good it did him."

"Don't overlook those bits of virtue you've acquired," she said. "You're not to blame for the way it turned out."

"Thanks."

"I believe that Julian might have had the right idea," she said. "I don't feel like staying awake any longer."

I rose with her, walked her to the door.

"I'm all right," she said. "Really."

"Sure?"

She nodded sharply.

"See you in the morning then."

"I hope so," she said. "Now you can talk about me."

She winked and went out.

I turned back, saw that Benedict and Llewella were approaching.

"Turning in?" I asked.

Benedict nodded.

"Might as well," Llewella said, and she kissed me on the cheek.

"What was that for?"

"A number of things," she said. "Good night."

"Good night."

Random was crouched on the hearth, poking at the fire. Deirdre turned to him and said, "Don't throw on more wood just for us. Flora and I are going too."

"Okay." He set the poker aside and rose. "Sleep well," he called after them.

Deirdre gave me a sleepy smile and Flora a nervous one. I added my good nights and watched them leave.

"Learn anything new and useful?" Random asked.

I shrugged.

"Did you?"

"Opinions, conjectures. No new facts," he said. "We were trying to decide who might be next on the list."

"And . . . ?"

"Benedict thinks it's a toss-up. You or him. Providing you are not behind it all, of course. He also thinks your buddy Ganelon ought to watch his step."

"Ganelon . . . Yes, that's a thought—and it should have been mine. I think he is right about the toss-up, too. It may even be slightly weighted against him, since they know I'm alert because of the attempted frameup."

"I would say that all of us are now aware that Benedict is alert himself. He managed to mention his opinion to everyone. I believe that he would welcome an attempt."

I chuckled.

"That balances the coin again. I guess it *is* a toss-up."

"He said that, too. Naturally, he knew I would tell you."

"Naturally, I wish he would start talking to me again. Well . . . not much I can do about it now," I said. "The hell with everything. I'm going to bed."

He nodded.

"Look under it first."

We left the room, headed up the hall.

"Corwin, I wish you'd had the foresight to bring some coffee back with you, along with the guns," he said. "I could use a cup."

"Doesn't it keep you awake?"

"No. I like a couple of cups in the evening."

"I miss it mornings. We'll have to import some when this mess is all settled."

"Small comfort, but a good idea. What got into Fi, anyhow?"

"She thinks Julian is our man."

"She may be right."

"What about Caine?"

"Supposing it was not a single individual," he said as we mounted the stair. "Say it was two, like Julian *and* Caine. They finally had a falling out, Caine lost, Julian disposed of him and used the death to weaken your position as well. Former friends make the worst enemies."

"It's no use," I said. "I get dizzy when I start sorting the possibilities. We are either going to have to wait for something more to happen, or make something happen. Probably the latter. But not tonight—"

"Hey! Wait up!"

"Sorry." I paused at the landing. "Don't know what got into me. Finishing spurt, I guess."

"Nervous energy," he said, coming abreast of me once more. We continued on up, and I made an effort to match his pace, fighting down a desire to hurry.

"Well, sleep well," he said finally.

"Good night, Random."

He continued on up the stair and I headed off along the corridor toward my quarters. I was feeling jittery by then, which must be why I dropped my key.

I reached and plucked it out of the air before it had fallen very far. Simultaneously, I was struck by the impression that its motion was somewhat slower than it should have been. I inserted it in the lock and turned it.

The room was dark, but I decided against lighting
a candle or an oil lamp. I had gotten used to the dark
a long time ago. I locked and bolted the door. My eyes
were already half adjusted to the gloom, from the dim
hallway. I turned. There was some starlight leaking in
about the drapes, too. I crossed the room, unfastening
my collar.

He was waiting in my bed chamber, to the left of the
entrance. He was perfectly positioned and he did nothing to give himself away. I walked right into it. He had
the ideal station, he held the dagger ready, he had the
element of total surprise going for him. By rights I
should have died—not in my bed, but just there at its
foot.

I caught a glimpse of the movement, realized the
presence and its significance as I stepped over the
threshold.

I knew that it was too late to avoid the thrust even as
I raised my arm to try to block it. But one peculiarity
struck me before the blade itself did: my assailant
seemed to be moving too slowly. Quick, with all the
tension of his wait behind it, that is how it should have
been. I should never have known it was occurring until
after the act, if then. I should not have had time to turn
partway and swing my arm as far as I did. A ruddy
haze filled my vision and I felt my forearm strike the
side of the outflung arm at about the same moment
as the steel touched my belly and bit. Within the
redness there seemed a faint tracing of that cosmic
version of the Pattern I had followed earlier in the day.
As I doubled and fell, unable to think but still for a
moment conscious, it came clearer, came nearer, the design. I wanted to flee, but horse my body stumbled. I
was thrown.

8

Out of every life a little blood must spill. Unfortunately, it was my turn again, and it felt like more than a little. I was lying, doubled up, on my right side, both arms clutching at my middle. I was wet, and every now and then something trickled along the creases of my belly. Front, lower left, just above the beltline, I felt like a casually opened envelope. These were my first sensations as consciousness came around again. And my first thought was, "What is he waiting for?" Obviously, the *coup de grâce* had been withheld. Why?

I opened my eyes. They had taken advantage of whatever time had elapsed to adjust themselves to the darkness. I turned my head. I did not see anyone else in the room with me. But something peculiar had occurred and I could not quite place it. I closed my eyes and let my head fall back to the mattress once more.

Something was wrong, yet at the same time right. . . .

The mattress . . . Yes, I was lying on my bed. I doubted my ability to have gotten there unassisted. But it would be absurd to knife me and then help me to bed.

My bed . . . It was my bed, yet it was not.

I squeezed my eyes tight. I gritted my teeth. I did not understand. I knew that my thinking could not be normal there on the fringes of shock, by blood pooling in my guts and then leaking out. I tried to force myself to think clearly. It was not easy.

My bed. Before you are fully aware of anything else,

you are aware whether you are awakening in your own bed. And I was, but—

I fought down an enormous impulse to sneeze, because I felt it would tear me apart. I compressed my nostrils and breathed in short gasps through my mouth. The taste, smell and feel of dust was all about me.

The nasal assault subsided and I opened my eyes. I knew then where I was. I did not understand the why and how of it, but I had come once more to a place I had never expected to see again.

I lowered my right hand, used it to raise myself.

It was my bedroom in my house. The old one. The place which had been mine back when I was Carl Corey. I had been returned to Shadow, to that world heavy with dust. The bed had not been made up since the last time I had slept in it, over half a decade before. I knew the state of the house fully, having looked in on it only a few weeks earlier.

I pushed myself further, managed to slide my feet out over the edge of the bed and down. Then I doubled up again and sat there. It was bad.

While I felt temporarily safe from further assault, I knew that I required more than safety just then. I had to have help, and I was in no position to help myself. I was not even certain how much longer I might remain conscious. So I had to get down and get out. The phone would be dead, the nearest house was not too close by. I would have to get down to the road, at least. I reflected grimly that one of my reasons for locating where I had was that it was not a well-traveled road. I enjoy my solitude, at least some of the time.

With my right hand I drew up the nearest pillow and slipped off its case. I turned it inside out, tried to fold it, gave up, wadded it, slipped it beneath my shirt, and pressed it against my wound. Then I sat there, just holding it in place. It had been a major exertion and I found it painful to take too deep a breath.

After a time, though, I drew the second pillow to me, held it across my knees and let it slip out of its case.

I wanted the pillowslip to wave at a passing motorist, for my garments, as usual, were dark. Before I could draw it through my belt, though, I was confounded by the behavior of the pillow itself. It had not yet reached the floor. I had released it, nothing was supporting it, and it *was* moving. But it was moving quite slowly, descending with a dreamlike deliberation.

I thought of the fall of the key as I had dropped it outside my room. I thought of my unintended quickness on mounting the stair with Random. I thought of Fiona's words, and of the Jewel of Judgment, which still hung about my neck now pulsating in time with the throbbing of my side. It might have saved my life, at least for the moment; yes, it probably had, if Fiona's notions were correct. It had probably given me a moment or so more than would otherwise have been my due when the assailant struck, letting me turn, letting me swing my arm. It might, somehow, even have been responsible for my sudden transportation. But I would have to think about such things at another time, should I succeed in maintaining a meaningful relationship with the future. For now, the jewel had to go—in case Fiona's fears concerning it were also correct—and I had to get moving.

I tucked away the second pillow cover, then tried to stand, holding on to the footboard. No good! Dizziness and too much pain. I lowered myself to the floor, afraid of passing out on the way down. I made it. I rested. Then I began to move, a slow crawl.

The front door, as I recalled, was now nailed shut. All right. Out the back, then.

I made it to the bedroom and halted, leaning against its frame. As I rested there I removed the Jewel of Judgment from my neck and wrapped its chain about my wrist. I had to cache it someplace, and the safe in my study was too far out of the way. Besides, I believed that I was leaving a trail of blood. Anyone finding and following it might well be curious enough to investigate and spring the small thing. And I lacked the time and the energy....

I made my way out, around, and through. I had to rise and exert myself to get the back door open. I made the mistake of not resting first.

When I regained consciousness, I was lying across the threshold. The night was raw and clouds filled much of the sky. A mean wind rattled branches above the patio. I felt several drops of moisture on the back of my out-flung hand.

I pushed up and crawled out. The snow was about two inches deep. The icy air helped to revive me. With something near panic, I realized just how foggy my mind had been during much of my course from the bedroom. It was possible that I might go under at any time.

I started immediately for the far corner of the house, deviating only to reach the compost heap, tear my way into it, drop the jewel, and reposition the clump of dead grasses I had broken loose. I brushed snow over it and continued on.

Once I made it about the corner, I was shielded from the wind and headed down a slight incline. I reached the front of the house and rested once more. A car had just passed and I watched its taillights dwindle. It was the only vehicle in sight.

Icy crystals stung my face as I moved again. My knees were wet and burning cold. The front yard sloped, gently at first, then dropped sharply toward the road. There was a dip about a hundred yards to the right, where motorists generally hit their brakes. It seemed that this might give me a few moments more in the headlights of anyone coming from that direction— one of those small assurances the mind always seeks when things get serious, an aspirin for the emotions. With three rest stops, I made it down to the roadside, then over to the big rock that bore my house number. I sat on it and leaned back against the icy embankment. I hauled out the second pillow case and draped it across my knees.

I waited. I knew that my mind was fuzzy. I believe that I drifted into and out of consciousness a number of times. Whenever I caught myself at it, I attempted to impose some version of order on my thoughts, to assess what had happened in the light of everything else that had just happened, to seek other safety measures. The former effort proved too much, however. It was simply too difficult to think beyond the level of responding to circumstance. With a sort of numb enlightenment, though, it occurred to me that I was still in possession of my Trumps. I could contact someone in Amber, have him transport me back.

But who? I was not so far gone that I failed to realize I might be contacting the one responsible for my condition. Would it be better to gamble that way, or to take my chances here? Still, Random or Gérard—

I thought that I heard a car. Faint, distant . . . The wind and my pulsebeat were competing wth perception, though. I turned my head. I concentrated.

There . . . Again. Yes. It was an engine. I got ready to wave the cloth.

Even then, my mind kept straying. And one thought that flitted through was that I might already be unable to muster sufficient concentration to manipulate the Trumps.

The sound grew louder. I raised the cloth. Moments later, the farthest visible point along the road to my right was touched with light. Shortly after, I saw the car at the top of the rise. I lost sight of it once more as it descended the hill. Then it climbed again and came on, snowflakes flashing through its headbeams.

I began waving as it approached the dip. The lights caught me as it came up out of it, and the driver could not have missed seeing me. He went by, though, a man in a late model sedan, a woman in the passenger seat. The woman turned and looked at me, but the driver did not even slow down.

A couple of minutes later another car came by, a bit older, a woman driving, no visible passengers. It did slow down, but only for a moment. She must not have liked my looks. She stepped on the gas and was gone in an instant.

I sagged back and rested. A prince of Amber can hardly invoke the brotherhood of man for purposes of moral condemnation. At least not with a straight face, and it hurt too much to laugh just then.

Without strength, concentration, and some ability to move, my power over Shadow was useless. I would use it first, I decided, to get to some warm place. . . . I wondered whether I could make it back up the hill, to the compost heap. I had not thought of trying to use the jewel to alter the weather. Probably I was too weak for that too, though. Probably the effort would kill me. Still . . .

I shook my head. I was drifting off, more than half a dream. I had to stay awake. Was that another car? Maybe. I tried to raise the cloth and dropped it. When I leaned forward to retrieve it, I just had to rest my head on my knees for a moment. Deirdre . . . I would call my dear sister. If anyone would help me, Deirdre would. I would get out her Trump and call her. In a minute. If only she weren't my sister . . . I had to rest. I am a knave, not a fool. Perhaps, sometimes, when I rest, I am even sorry for things. Some things. If only it were warmer . . . But it wasn't too bad, bent over this way . . . Was that a car? I wanted to raise my head but found that I could not. It would not make that much difference in being seen, though, I decided.

I felt light on my eyelids and I heard the engine. Now it was neither advancing nor retreating. Just a steady cycling of growls. Then I heard a shout. Then the click-pause-chunk of a car door opening and closing. I felt that I could open my eyes but I did not want to. I was afraid that I would look only on the dark and empty road, that the sounds would resolve into pulse-beats and wind once more. It was better to keep what I had than to gamble.

"Hey! What's the matter? You hurt?"

Footsteps . . . This was real.

I opened my eyes. I forced myself up once again.

"Corey! My God! It's *you!*"

I forced a grin, cut my nod short of a topple.

"It's me, Bill. How've you been?"

"What happened?"

"I'm hurt," I said. "Maybe bad. Need a doctor."

"Can you walk if I help? Or should I carry you?"

"Let's try walking," I said.

He got me to my feet and I leaned on him. We started for his car. I only remember the first few steps.

When that low-swinging sweet chariot turned sour and swung high once more, I tried to raise my arm, realized that it was restrained, settled for a consideration of the tube affixed thereto, and decided that I was going to live. I had sniffed hospital smells and consulted my internal clock. Having made it this far, I felt that I owed it to myself to continue. And I was warm, and as comfortable as recent history allowed. That settled, I closed my eyes, lowered my head, and went back to sleep.

Later, when I came around again, felt more fit and was spotted by a nurse, she told me that it was seven hours since I had been brought in and that a doctor would be by to talk with me shortly. She also got me a glass of water and told me that it had stopped snowing. She was curious as to what had happened to me.

I decided that it was time to start plotting my story. The simpler the better. All right. I was coming home after an extended stay abroad. I had hitchhiked out, gone on in, and been attacked by some vandal or drifter I had surprised inside. I crawled back out and sought help. Finis.

When I told it to the doctor I could not tell at first whether he believed me. He was a heavy man whose face had sagged and set long ago. His name was Bailey, Morris Bailey, and he nodded as I spoke and then asked me, "Did you get a look at the fellow?"

I shook my head.

"It was dark," I said.

"Did he rob you too?"

"I don't know."

"Were you carrying a wallet?"

I decided I had better say yes to that one.

"Well, you didn't have it when you came in here, so he must have taken it."

"Must have," I agreed.

"Do you remember me at all?"

"Can't say that I do. Should I?"

"You seemed vaguely familiar to me when they brought you in. That was all, at first . . ."

"And . . . ?" I asked.

"What sort of garments were you wearing? They seemed something like a uniform."

"Latest thing, Over There, these days. You were saying that I looked familiar?"

"Yes," he agreed. "Where is Over There, anyway? Where did you come from? Where have you been?"

"I travel a lot," I said. "You were going to tell me something a moment ago."

"Yes," he said. "We are a small clinic, and some time ago a fast-talking salesman persuaded the directors to invest in a computerized medical-records system. If the area had developed more and we had expanded a lot, it might have been worthwhile. Neither of these things happened, though, and it is an expensive item. It even encouraged a certain laziness among the clerical help. Old files just don't get purged the way they used to, even for the emergency room. Space there for a lot of useless backlog. So, when Mr. Roth gave me your name and I ran a routine check on you, I found something and I realized why you looked familiar. I had been working the emergency room that night too, around seven years ago, when you had your auto accident. I remembered working on you then—and how I thought you weren't going to make it. You surprised me, though, and you still do. I can't even find the scars that *should* be there. You did a nice job of healing up."

"Thanks. A tribute to the physician, I'd say."

"May I have your age, for the record?"

"Thirty-six," I said. That's always safe.

He jotted it somewhere in the folder he held across his knees.

"You know, I would have sworn—once I got to checking you over and remembering—that that's about what you looked the last time I saw you."

"Clean living."

"Do you know about your blood type?"

"It's an exotic. But you can treat it as an AB positive for all practical purposes. I can take anything, but don't give mine to anybody else."

He nodded.

"The nature of your mishap is going to require a police report, you know."

"I had guessed that."

"Just thought you might want to be thinking about it."

"Thanks," I said. "So you were on duty that night, and you patched me up? Interesting. What else do you recall about it?"

"What do you mean?"

"The circumstances under which I was brought in that time. My own memory is a blank from right before the accident until some time after I had been transferred up to the other place—Greenwood. Do you recall how I arrived?"

He frowned, just when I had decided he had one face for all occasions.

"We sent an ambulance," he said.

"In response to what? Who reported the accident? How?"

"I see what you mean," he said. "It was the State Patrol that called for the ambulance. As I recollect, someone had seen the accident and phoned their headquarters. They then radioed a car in the vicinity. It went to the lake, verified the report, gave you first aid, and called for the ambulance. And that was it."

"Any record of who called in the report in the first place?"

He shrugged.

"That's not the sort of thing we keep track of," he said. "Didn't your insurance company investigate? Wasn't there a claim? They could probably——"

"I had to leave the country right after I recovered," I said. "I never pursued the matter. I suppose there would have been a police report, though."

"Surely. But I have no idea how long they keep them around." He chuckled. "Unless, of course, that same salesman got to them, too. . . . It is rather late to be talking about that though, isn't it? It seems to me there is a statute of limitations on things of that sort. Your friend Roth will tell you for sure——"

"It isn't a claim that I have in mind," I said. "Just a desire to know what really happened. I have wondered about it on and off for a number of years now. You see, I have this touch of retrograde amnesia going."

"Have you ever talked it over with a psychiatrist?" he said, and there was something about the way he said it that I did not like. Came one of those little flashes of insight then: Could Flora have managed to get me certified insane before my transfer to Greenwood? Was that on my record here? And was I still on escape status from that place? A lot of time had passed and I knew nothing of the legalities involved. If this was indeed the case, however, I imagined they would have no way of knowing whether I had been certified sane again in some other jurisdiction. Prudence, I guess it was, cautioned me to lean forward and glance at the doctor's wrist. I seemed possessed of a subliminal memory that he had consulted a calendar watch when taking my pulse. Yes, he had, I squinted. All right. Day and month: November 28. I did a quick calculation with my two-and-a-half-to-one conversion and had the year. It *was* seven, as he had indicated.

"No, I haven't," I said. "I just assumed it was organic rather than functional and wrote the time off as a loss."

"I see," he said. "You use such phrases rather glibly. People who've been in therapy sometimes do that."

"I know," I said. "I've read a lot about it."

He sighed. He stood.

"Look," he said. "I am going to call Mr. Roth and let him know you are awake. It is probably best."

"What do you mean by that?"

"I mean that with your friend being an attorney, there might be things you want to discuss with him before you talk to the police."

He opened the folder wherein he had somewhere jotted my age, raised his pen, furrowed his brow, and said, "What's the date, anyway?"

I wanted my Trumps. I imagined my belongings would be in the drawer of the bedside table, but getting at it involved too much twisting and I did not want to put the strain on my sutures. It was not all that urgent, though. Eight hours' sleep in Amber would come to around twenty hours here, so everyone should still have been respectably retired back home. I wanted to get hold of Random, though, to come up with some sort of cover story for my not being there in the morning. Later.

I did not want to look suspicious at a time like this. Also, I wanted to know immediately whatever Brand had to say. I wanted to be in a position to act on it. I did a quick bit of mental juggling. If I could do the worst of my recovering here in Shadow, it would mean less wasted time for me back in Amber. I would have to budget my time carefully and avoid complications on this end. I hoped that Bill would arrive soon. I was anxious to know what the picture was in this place.

Bill was a native of the area, had gone to school in Buffalo, come back, married, joined the family firm, and that was that. He had known me as a retired Army officer who sometimes traveled on vague business. We both belonged to the country club, which was where I had met him. I had known him for over a year without our exchanging more than a few words. Then one evening I happened to be next to him in the bar and it had somehow come out that he was hot on military history, particularly the Napoleonic Wars. The next thing we knew, they were closing up the place around us. We were close friends from then on, right up until the time of my difficulties. I had occasionally wondered about him since. In fact, the only thing that had prevented me from seeing him the last time I had passed through was that he would doubtless have had all sorts of questions as to what had become of me, and I had had too many things on my mind to deal with them all that gracefully and still enjoy myself. I had even thought once or twice of coming back and seeing him if I could, when everything was finally settled in Amber. Next to the fact that this was not the case, I regretted not being able to meet him in the club lounge.

He arrived within the hour, short, heavy, ruddy, a bit grayer on the sides, grinning, nodding. I had propped myself up by then, already tried a few deep breaths and decided they were premature. He clasped my hand and took the bedside chair. He had his briefcase with him.

"You scared the hell out of me last night, Carl. Thought I was seeing a ghost," he said.

I nodded.

"A bit later, and I might have been one," I said. "Thanks. How have you been?"

Bill sighed.

"Busy. You know. The same old stuff, only more of it."

"And Alice?"

"She's fine. And we've got two new grandsons—Bill Jr.'s—twins. Wait a minute."

He fished out his wallet and located a photo.

"Here."

I studied it, noted the family resemblances.

"Hard to believe," I said.

"You don't look much worse for the years."

I chuckled and patted my abdomen.

"Subtracting that, I mean," he said. "Where have you been?"

"God! Where haven't I been!" I said. "So many places I've lost count."

He remained expressionless, caught my eyes and stared.

"Carl, what kind of trouble are you in?" he asked.

I smiled.

"If you mean am I in trouble with the law, the answer is no. My troubles actually involve another country, and I am going to have to go back there shortly."

His face relaxed again, and there was a small glint behind his bifocals.

"Are you some sort of military adviser in that place?"

I nodded.

"Can you tell me where?"

I shook my head.

"Sorry."

"That I can sort of understand," he said. "Dr. Roth told me what you said had happened last night. Off the record now, was it connected with whatever you have been doing?"

I nodded again.

"That makes things a little clearer," he said. "Not much, but enough. I won't even ask you which agency, or even if there is one. I have always known you to be a gentleman, and a rational one at that. That was why I grew curious at the time of your disappearance and did some investigating. I felt a bit officious and self-conscious about it. But your civil status was quite puzzling, and I wanted to know what had happened. Mainly, because I was concerned about you. I hope that doesn't disturb you."

"Disturb me?" I said. "There aren't that many people who care what happens to me. I'm grateful. Also, curious what you discovered. I never had the time to look into it, you know, to straighten things out. How about telling me what you learned?"

He opened the briefcase and withdrew a manila folder. Spreading it across his knees, he shuffled out several sheets of yellow paper covered with neat handwriting. Raising the first of these, he regarded it a moment, then said, "After you escaped from the hospital in Albany and had your accident, Brandon apparently dropped out of the picture and—"

"Stop!" I said, raising my hand, trying to sit up.

"What?" he asked.

"You have the order wrong, also the place," I said. "First came the accident, and Greenwood is not in Albany."

"I know," he said. "I was referring to the Porter Sanitarium, where you spent two days and then escaped. You had your accident that same day, and you were brought here as a result of it. Then your sister Evelyn entered the picture. She had you transferred to Greenwood, where you spent a couple of weeks before departing on your own motion once again. Right?"

"Partly," I said. "Namely, the last part. As I was telling the doctor earlier, my memory is shot for a couple of days prior to the accident. This business about a place in Albany *does* sort of seem to ring a bell, but only very faintly. Do you have more on it?"

"Oh yes," he said. "It may even have something to do with the state of your memory. You were committed on a bum order—"

"By whom?"

He shook the paper and peered.

" 'Brother, Brandon Corey; attendant physician, Hillary B. Rand, psychiatrist,' " he read. "Hear any more bells?"

"Quite possibly," I said. "Go ahead."

"Well, an order got signed on that basis," he said. "You were duly certified, taken into custody, and transported. Then, concerning your memory . . ."

"Yes?"

"I don't know that much about the practice and its effects on the memory, but you were subjected to electroshock therapy while you were at Porter. Then, as I said, the record indicates that you escaped after the second day. You apparently recovered your car from some unspecified locale and were heading back this way when you had the accident."

"That seems right," I said. "It does." For a moment, when he had begun talking, I had had a wild vision of having been returned to the wrong shadow—one where everything was similar, but not congruent. Now, though, I did not believe this to be the case. I was responding to this story on some level.

"Now, about that order," he said. "It was based on false evidence, but there was no way of the court's knowing it at the time. The real Dr. Rand was in England when everything happened, and when I contacted him later he had never heard of you. His office had been broken into while he was away, though. Also, peculiarly, his middle initial is not B. He had never heard of Brandon Corey either."

"What did become of Brandon?"

"He simply vanished. Several attempts were made to contact him at the time of your escape from Porter, but he could not be found. Then you had the accident, were brought here and treated. At that time, a woman named Evelyn Flaumel, who represented herself as your sister, contacted this place, told them you had been probated and that the family wanted you transferred to Greenwood. In the absence of Brandon, who had been appointed your guardian, her instructions were followed, as the only available next of kin. That was how it came about that you were sent to the other place. You escaped again, a couple of weeks later, and that is where my chronology ends."

"Then what is my legal status right now?" I asked.

"Oh, you've been made whole," he said. "Dr. Rand went down after I talked with him and gave the court an affidavit reciting these facts. The order was vacated."

"Then why is the doctor here acting as if I might be a psycho case?"

"Oh my! That *is* a thought. It hadn't occurred to me. All their records here would show is that one time you apparently were. I had better see him on the way out. I have a copy of the journal entry in here, too. I can show it to him."

"How long was it after I left Greenwood that things were set right with the court?"

"The following month," he said. "It was several weeks before I could bring myself to get nosy."

"You couldn't know how happy I am that you did," I said. "And you have given me several pieces of information I think are going to prove extremely important."

"It is nice to be able to help a friend sometime," he said, closing the folder and replacing it in his briefcase. "One thing . . . When this is all over—whatever you are doing—if you are permitted to talk about it, I would like to hear the story."

"I can't promise," I said.

"I know. Just thought I'd mention it. By the way, what do you want to do about the house?"

"Mine? Do I still hold title to it?"

"Yes, but it will probably be sold this year for back taxes if you don't do anything about it."

"I'm surprised that hasn't already happened."

"You gave the bank power of attorney for paying your bills."

"I never thought of that. I'd just set it up for utilities and my charge accounts. Stuff like that."

"Well, the account is nearly empty now," he said. "I was talking to McNally over there the other day. That means the house will go next year if you don't do anything."

"I've got no use for it now," I said. "They can do whatever they want with it."

"Then you might as well sell it and realize what you can."

"I won't be around that long."

"I could handle it for you. Send the money wherever you want."

"All right," I said. "I'll sign anything necessary. Pay my hospital bill out of it and keep the rest."

"I couldn't do that."

I shrugged.

"Do whatever you think best, but be sure and take a good fee."

"I'll put the balance in your account."

"All right. Thanks. By the way, before I forget, would you look in the drawer of that table and see if there is a deck of cards there? I can't reach it yet, and I'll be wanting them later."

"Surely."

He reached over, opened it.

"A big brown envelope," he said. "Kind of bulgy. They probably put whatever was in your pockets in it."

"Open it."

"Yes, here's a pack of cards," he said, reaching inside. "Say! That's a beautiful case! May I?"

"I—" What could I say?

He slipped the case.

"Lovely . . ." he murmured. "Some kind of tarots . . . Are they antique?"

"Yes."

"Cold as ice . . . I never saw anything like these. Say, that's you! Dressed up like some kind of knight! What's their purpose?"

"A very complicated game," I said.

"How could that be you if they are antique?"

"I didn't say it was me. You did."

"Yes, so I did. Ancestor?"

"Sort of."

"Now that's a good-looking gal! But so is the red-head. . . ."

"I think . . ."

He squared the deck and replaced it in the case. He passed it to me.

"Nice unicorn, too," he added. "I shouldn't have looked at them, should I?"

"That's all right."

He sighed and leaned back in the chair, clasping his hands behind his head.

"I couldn't help it," he said. "It is just that there is something very strange about you, Carl, beyond any hush-hush work you may be doing—and mysteries intrigue me. I've never been this close to a real puzzler before."

"Because you just slipped yourself a cold deck of tarots?" I asked.

"No, that just adds atmosphere," he said. "While what you have been doing all these years is admittedly none of my business, there is one recent incident I am unable to comprehend."

"What is that?"

"After I brought you here and took Alice home last night, I went back to your place, hoping to get some sort of idea as to what had happened. The snow had let up by then, though it started in again later, and your track was still clearly visible, going around the house and down the front yard."

I nodded.

"But there were no tracks going in—nothing to indicate your arrival. And for that matter, there were no other tracks departing—nothing to show the flight of your assailant."

I chuckled.

"You think the wound was self-inflicted?"

"No, of course not. There wasn't even a weapon in sight. I followed the bloodstains back to the bedroom, to your bed. I had only my flashlight to see by, of course, but what I saw gave me an eerie feeling. It seemed as if you had just suddenly appeared there on the bed, bleeding, and then gotten up and made your way out."

"Impossible, of course."

"I wonder about the lack of tracks, though."

"The wind must have blown snow over them."

"And not the others?" He shook his head. "No, I don't think so. I just want to go on the record as interested in the answer to that one too, if you ever do want to tell me about things."

"I will remember," I said.

"Yes," he said. "But I wonder . . . I've a peculiar feeling that I may never see you again. It is as if I were one of those minor characters in a melodrama who gets shuffled offstage without ever learning how things turn out."

"I can appreciate the feeling," I said. "My own role sometimes makes me want to strangle the author. But look at it this way: inside stories seldom live up to one's expectations. Usually they are grubby little things, reducing down to the basest of motives when all is known. Conjectures and illusions are often the better possessions."

He smiled.

"You talk the same as always," he said, "yet I have known occasions when you have been tempted to virtue. Several of them . . ."

"How did we get from the footprints to me?" I said. "I was about to tell you that I suddenly recalled having approached the house by exactly the same route as I left it. My departure obviously obliterated the signs of my arrival."

"Not bad," he said. "And your attacker followed the same route?"

"Must have."

"Pretty good," he acknowledged. "You know how to raise a reasonable doubt. But I still feel that the preponderance of evidence indicates the weird."

"Weird? No. Peculiar, perhaps. A matter of interpretation."

"Or semantics. Have you read the police report on your accident?"

"No. Have you?"

"Uh-huh. What if *it* was more than peculiar? Then

will you grant me my word, as I used it: 'weird'?"

"Very well."

". . . And answer one question?"

"I don't know. . . ."

"A simple yes-or-no question. That's all."

"Okay, it's a deal. What did it say?"

"It said that they received report of the accident and a patrol car proceeded to the scene. There they encountered a strangely garbed man in the process of giving you first aid. He stated that he had pulled you from the wrecked car in the lake. This seemed believable in that he was also soaking wet. Average height, light build, red hair. He had on a green outfit that one of the officers said looked like something out of a Robin Hood movie. He refused to identify himself, to accompany them or to give a statement of any sort. When they insisted that he do so, he whistled and a white horse came trotting up. He leaped onto its back and rode off. He was not seen again."

I laughed. It hurt, but I couldn't help it.

"I'll be damned!" I said. "Things are starting to make sense."

Bill just stared at me for a moment. Then, "Really?" he said.

"Yes, I think so. It may well have been worth getting stabbed and coming back for what I learned today."

"You put the two in peculiar order," he said, massaging his chin.

"Yes, I do. But I am beginning to see some order where I had seen nothing before. This one may have been worth the price of admission, all unintended."

"All because of a guy on a white horse?"

"Partly, partly . . . Bill, I am going to be leaving here soon."

"You are not going anywhere for a while."

"Just the same—those papers you mentioned . . . I think I had better get them signed today."

"All right. I'll get them over this afternoon. But I don't want you doing anything foolish."

"I grow more cautious by the moment," I said, "believe me."

"I hope so," he said, snapping his briefcase shut and rising. "Well, get your rest. I'll clear things up with the doctor and have those papers sent over today."

"Thanks again."

I shook his hand.

"By the way," he said, "you did agree to answer a question."

"I did, didn't I? What is it?"

"Are you human?" he asked, still gripping my hand, no special expression on his face.

I started in on a grin, then threw it away.

"I don't know. I—I like to think so. But I don't really —Of course I am! That's a silly . . . Oh hell! You really mean it, don't you? And I said I'd be honest. . . ." I chewed my lip and thought for a moment. Then, "I don't think so," I said.

"Neither do I," he said, and he smiled. "It doesn't make any real difference to me, but I thought it might to you—to know that someone knows you are different and doesn't care."

"I'll remember that, too," I said.

"Well . . . see you around."

"Right."

9

It was just after the state patrolman left . . . Late afternoon. I was lying there feeling better, and feeling better that I felt better. Lying there, reflecting on the hazards involved in living in Amber. Brand and I were both laid up by means of the family's favorite weapon. I wondered who had gotten it worse. Probably he had. It might have reached his kidney, and he was in poor condition to begin with.

I had stumbled across the room and back again twice before Bill's clerk came over with the papers for me to sign. It was necessary that I know my limits. It always is. Since I tended to heal several times faster than those about me in that shadow, I felt that I ought to be able to stand and walk some, to perform in the same fashion as one of these after, say, a day and a half, maybe two. I established that I could. It did hurt, and I was dizzy the first time, less dizzy the second. That was something, anyway. So I lay there feeling better.

I had fanned the Trumps dozens of times, dealt private solitaires, read ambiguous fortunes among familiar faces. And each time I had restrained myself, suppressing my desire to contact Random, to tell him what had happened, to inquire after new developments. Later, I kept telling myself. Each additional hour they sleep is two and a half for you, here. Each two and a half for you, here, is the equivalent of seven or eight for some lesser mortal, here. Abide. Think. Regenerate.

And so it came to pass that a little after dinnertime, just as the sky was darkening again, I was beaten to the punch. I had already told a well-starched young member of the State Patrol everything that I was going to tell him. I have no idea whether he believed me, but he was polite and he did not stay long. In fact, it was only moments after he left that things began to happen.

Lying there, feeling better, I was waiting for Dr. Bailey to stop by and check whether I was still oriented. Lying there, assessing all of the things Bill had told me, trying to fit them together with other things that I knew or had guessed at. . . .

Contact! I had been anticipated. Someone in Amber was an early riser.

"Corwin!"

It was Random, agitated.

"Corwin! Get up! Open the door! Brand's come around, and he's asking for you."

"Have you been pounding on that door, trying to get me up?"

"That's right."

"Are you alone?"

"Yes."

"Good. I am not inside. You have reached me in Shadow."

"I do not understand."

"Neither do I. I am hurt, but I will live. I will give you the story later. Tell me about Brand."

"He woke up just a little while ago. Told Gérard he had to talk to you right away. Gérard rang up a servant, sent him to your room. When he couldn't rouse you, he came to me. I just sent him back to tell Gérard I'd be bringing you along shortly."

"I see," I said, stretching slowly and sitting up. "Get in some place where you can't be seen, and I'll come through. I will need a robe or something. I am missing some clothes."

"It could probably be best if I went back to my rooms, then."

"Okay. Go ahead."

"A minute, then."

And silence.

I moved my legs slowly. I sat on the edge of the bed. I gathered up my Trumps and replaced them in their case. I felt it important that I mask my injury back in Amber. Even in normal times one never advertises one's vulnerability.

I took a deep breath and stood, holding on to the bed frame. My practice had paid off. I breathed normally and relaxed my grip. Not bad, if I moved slowly, if I did not exert myself beyond the barest essentials required for appearances' sake . . . I might be able to carry it until my strength really returned.

Just then I heard a footfall, and a friendly nurse was framed in the doorway, crisp, symmetrical, differing from a snowflake mainly in that they are all of them alike.

"Get back in that bed, Mr. Corey! You are not supposed to be up!"

"Madam," I said, "it is quite necessary that I be up. I have to go."

"You could have rung for a pan," she said, entering the room and advancing.

I gave my head a weary shake just as Random's presence reached me once more. I wondered how she would report this one—and if she would mention my prismatic afterimage as I trumped out. Another entry, I suppose, for the growing record of folklore I tend to leave behind.

"Think of it this way, my dear," I told her. "Ours has been a purely physical relationship all along. There will be others . . . many others. *Adieu!*"

I bowed and blew her a kiss as I stepped forward into Amber, leaving her to clutch at rainbows as I caught hold of Random's shoulder and staggered.

"Corwin! What the hell—"

"If blood be the price of admiralty, I've just bought me a naval commission," I said. "Give me something to wear."

He draped a long, heavy cloak about my shoulders and I fumbled to clasp it at my throat.

"All set," I said. "Take me to him."

He led me out the door, into the hall, toward the stair. I leaned on him heavily as we went.

"How bad is it?" he asked me.

"Knife," I said, and laid my hand on the spot. "Someone attacked me in my room last night."

"Who?"

"Well, it couldn't have been you, because I had just left you," I said, "and Gérard was up in the library with Brand. Subtract the three of you from the rest and start guessing. That is the best—"

"Julian," he said.

"His stock is definitely bearish," I said. "Fiona was just running him down for me the other night, and of course it is no secret that he is not my favorite."

"Corwin, he's gone. He cut out during the night. The servant who came to get me told me that Julian had departed. What does that look like to you?"

We reached the stair. I kept one hand on Random and rested there briefly.

"I don't know," I said. "It can sometimes be just as bad to extend the benefit of the doubt too far as not to grant it at all. But it does occur to me that if he thought he had disposed of me, he would look a lot better by staying here and acting surprised to learn of it than by getting the hell out. That *does* look suspicious. I am inclined to think he might have departed because he was afraid of what Brand would have to say when he came around."

"But you lived, Corwin. You got away from whoever attacked you, and he could not be certain he had done you in. If it were me, I would be worlds away by now."

"There is that," I acknowledged, and we started on down again. "Yes, you might well be right. Let us leave it academic for now. And no one is to know I have been injured."

He nodded.

"As you say. Silence beats a chamber pot in Amber."

"How's that?"

" 'Tis gilt, m'lord, like a royal flush."

"Your wit pains both wounded and unwounded parts, Random. Spend some figuring how the assailant entered my room."

"Your panel?"

"It secures from the inside. I keep it that way now. And the door's lock is a new one. Tricky."

"All right, I have it. My answer requires that it be a family member, too."

"Tell me."

"Someone was willing to psyche himself up and tough it through the Pattern again for a shot at you. He went below, walked it, projected himself into your room, and attacked you."

"That would be perfect except for one thing. We all left at pretty much the same time. The attack did not occur later on in the evening. It happened immediately on my entering. I do not believe there was sufficient time for one of us to get down to the chamber, let alone negotiate the Pattern. The attacker was already waiting. So if it was one of us, he had gotten in by some other means."

"Then he picked your lock, tricks and all."

"Possibly," I said as we reached the landing and continued on. "We will rest at the corner so that I can go on into the library unassisted."

"Sure thing."

We did that. I composed myself, drew the cloak completely about me, squared my shoulders, advanced, and knocked on the door.

"Just a minute." Gérard's voice.

Footsteps approaching the door . . .

"Who is it?"

"Corwin," I said. "Random's with me."

I heard him call back, "You want Random, too?" and I heard a soft "No" in reply.

The door opened.

"Just you, Corwin," Gérard said.

I nodded and turned to Random.

"Later," I told him.

He returned my nod and headed back in the direction from which we had come. I entered the library.

"Open your cloak, Corwin," Gérard ordered.

"That is not necessary," Brand said, and I looked over and saw that he was propped up by a number of cushions and showing a yellow-toothed smile.

"Sorry, I am not as trusting as Brand," Gérard said, "and I will not have my work wasted. Let's have a look."

"I said that it is not necessary," Brand repeated. "He is not the one who stabbed me."

Gérard turned quickly.

"How do you know he isn't?" he asked.

"Because I know who did, of course. Don't be an ass, Gérard. I wouldn't have asked for him if I had reason to fear him."

"You were unconscious when I brought you through. You couldn't know who did it."

"Are you certain of that?"

"Well . . . Why didn't you tell me, then?"

"I have my reasons, and they are valid ones. I want to speak with Corwin alone now."

Gérard lowered his head.

"You had better not be delirious," he said. He stepped to the door, opened it again. "I'll be within hailing distance," he added, and closed it behind him.

I moved nearer. Brand reached up and I clasped his hand.

"Good to see that you made it back," he said.

"Vice versa," I said, and then I took Gérard's chair, trying not to collapse into it.

"How do you feel now?" I asked.

"Rotten, in one sense. But better than I have in years, in another. It's all relative."

"Most things are."

"Not Amber."

I sighed.

"All right. I wasn't getting technical. What the hell happened?"

His gaze was most intense. He was studying me, looking for something. What? Knowledge, I'd guess. Or, more correctly, ignorance. Negatives being harder to gauge, his mind had to be moving fast, must have been from the moment he had come around. Knowing him, he was more interested in what I did not know than in what I knew. He wasn't going to give away anything if he could help it. He wanted to know the minimum enlightenment he need shed in order to get what he wanted. Not a watt more would he willingly spend. For this was his way, and of course he wanted something. Unless . . . More strongly in recent years than ever before I have tried to convince myself that people do change, that the passage of time does not serve merely to accentuate that which is already there, that qualitative changes do sometimes occur in people because of things they have done, seen, thought, and felt. It would provide some small solace in times such as these when everything else seems to be going wrong, not to mention pepping up my mundane philosophy no end. And Brand had probably been responsible for saving my life and my memory, whatever his reasons. Very well, I resolved to give him the doubt's benefit without exposing my back. A small concession here, my move against the simple psychology of humors which generally governs the openings of our games.

"Things are never what they seem, Corwin," he began. "Your friend today is your enemy tomorrow, and—"

"Cut it out!" I said. "Cards-on-the-table time is here. I do appreciate what Brandon Corey did for me, and it was my idea to try the trick we used to locate you and bring you back."

He nodded.

"I fancy there were good reasons for a recrudescence of fraternal sentiment after all this time."

"I might suppose you had additional reasons for helping me, also."

He smiled again, raised his right hand and lowered it.

"Then we are either even or in each other's debt, depending upon how one looks at these things. As it would seem we now have need of each other, it would be well to regard ourselves in the most flattering light."

"You are stalling, Brand. You are trying to psych me. You are also spoiling my day's effort at idealism. You got me out of bed to tell me something. Be my guest."

"Same old Corwin," he said, chuckling. Then he looked away. "Or are you? I wonder . . . Did it change you, do you think? Living all that while in Shadow? Not knowing who you really were? Being a part of something else?"

"Maybe," I said. "I don't know. Yes, I guess I did. I know that it shortened my temper when it comes to family politics."

"Plain-speaking, blunt, plain-dealing? You miss some of the fun that way. But then there is a value to such novelty. Keep everyone unbalanced with it . . . revert when they least expect it. . . . Yes, it might prove valuable. Refreshing, too. All right! Panic not. Thus end my preliminaries. All pleasantries are now exchanged. I'll bare the basics, bridle the beast Unreason, and wrest from murky mystery the pearl of sweetest sense. But one thing first, if you would. Have you anything smokable with you? It has been a number of years, and I'd like some foul weed or other—to celebrate my homecoming."

I started to say no. But I was sure there were some cigarettes in the desk, left there by me. I did not really want the exercise, but, "Just a minute," I said.

I tried to make my movements look casual rather than stiff as I rose and crossed the room. I attempted to make it seem as if I were resting my hand naturally upon the desktop as I rummaged through it, rather than leaning as heavily as I was. I masked my movements with my body and my cloak as much as possible.

I located the package and returned as I had come, stopping to light a pair at the hearth. Brand was slow in taking his from me.

"Your hand is rather shaky," he said. "What is the matter?"

"Too much partying last night," I said, returning to my chair.

"I hadn't thought of that. I imagine there would have been, wouldn't there? Of course. Everyone together in one room . . . Unexpected success in finding me, bringing me back . . . A desperate move on the part of a very nervous, very guilty person. . . . Half success there. Me injured and mum, but for how long? Then—"

"You said that you knew who did it. Were you kidding?"

"No, I was not."

"Who then?"

"In its place, dear brother. In its place. Sequence and order, time and stress—they are most important in this matter. Allow me to savor the drama of the event in safe retrospect. I see me punctured and all of you gathered round. Ah! what would I not give to witness that tableau! Could you possibly describe for me the expression on each face?"

"I'm afraid their faces were my least concern at the time."

He sighed and blew smoke.

"Ah, that is good," he said. "Never mind, I can see their faces. I've a vivid imagination, you know. Shock, distress, puzzlement—shading over into suspicion, fear. Then all of you departed, I'm told, and gentle Gérard my nursemaid here." He paused, stared into the smoke, and for a moment the note of mockery was absent. "He is the only decent one among us, you know."

"He's high on my list," I said.

"He took good care of me. He's always looked out

for the rest of us." He chuckled suddenly. "Frankly, I can't see why he bothers. As I was musing, though—prompted by your recuperating self—you must have adjourned to talk things over. There is another party I'm sad I missed. All those emotions and suspicions and lies bouncing off one another—and no one wanting to be the first to say good night. It must have gotten shrill after a time. Everyone on his own best behavior, with an eye out to blacken the rest. Attempts to intimidate the one guilty person. Perhaps a few stones shied at scapegoats. But, all in all, nothing much really accomplished. Am I right?"

I nodded, appreciative of the way his mind worked, and resigned to letting him tell it his way.

"You know you're right," I said.

He gave me a sharp look at that, then went on. "But everyone did finally go off, to lie awake worrying, or to get together with an accomplice, to scheme. There were hidden turmoils in the night. It is flattering to know that my well-being was on everyone's mind. Some, of course, were for it, others against. And in the midst of it all, I rallied—nay, flourished—not wishing to disappoint my supporters. Gérard spent a long while bringing me up to date on recent history. When I had enough of this, I sent for you."

"In case you haven't noticed, I'm here. What did you want to tell me?"

"Patience, brother! Patience! Consider all the years you spent in Shadow, not even remembering—this." He gestured widely with his cigarette. "Consider all that time you waited, unknowing, until I succeeded in locating you and tried to remedy your plight. Surely a few moments now are not so priceless by contrast."

"I was told that you had sought me," I said. "I wondered at that, for we had not exactly parted on the best of terms the last time we were together."

He nodded.

"I cannot deny it," he said. "But I always get over such things, eventually."

I snorted.

"I have been deciding how much to tell you, and what you would believe," he continued. "I doubted you would accept it if I had simply come out and said that, save for a few small items, my present motives are almost entirely altruistic."

I snorted again.

"But this is true," he went on, "and to lay your suspicions, I add that it is because I have small choice in it. Beginnings are always difficult. Wherever I begin, something preceded it. You were gone for so long. If one must name a single thing, however, then let it be the throne. There. I have said it. We had thought of a way to take it, you see. This was just after your disappearance, and in some ways, I suppose, prompted by it. Dad suspected Eric of having slain you. But there was no evidence. We worked on this feeling, though— a word here and there, every now and then. Years passed, with you unreachable by any means, and it seemed more and more likely that you were indeed dead. Dad looked upon Eric with growing disfavor. Then, one night, pursuant to a discussion I had begun on a totally neutral matter—most of us present at the table—he said that no fratricide would ever take the throne, and he was looking at Eric as he said it. You know how his eyes could get. Eric grew bright as a sunset and could not swallow for a long while. But then Dad took things much further than any of us had anticipated or desired. In fairness to you, I do not know whether he spoke solely to vent his feelings, or whether he actually meant what he said. But he told us that he had more than half decided upon you as his successor, so that he took whatever misadventure had befallen you quite personally. He would not have spoken of it, but that he was convinced as to your passing. In the months that followed, we reared you a cenotaph to give some solid form to this conclusion, and we made certain that no one forgot Dad's feelings toward Eric. All along, after yourself, Eric was the one we felt had to be gotten around to reach the throne."

"We! Who were the others?"

"Patience, Corwin. Sequence and order, time and stress! Accent, emphasis . . . Listen." He took another cigarette, chain-lit it from the butt, stabbed the air with its burning tip. "The next step required that we get Dad out of Amber. This was the most crucial and dangerous part of it, and it was here that we disagreed. I did not like the idea of an alliance with a power I did not fully understand, especially one that gave them some hold on us. Using shadows is one thing; allowing them to use you is ill-considered, whatever the circumstances. I argued against it, but the majority had it otherwise." He smiled. "Two to one. Yes, there were three of us. We went ahead then. The trap was set and Dad went after the bait—"

"Is he still living?" I asked.

"I do not know," Brand said. "Things went wrong afterward, and then I'd troubles of my own to concern me. After Dad's departure, though, our next move was to consolidate our position while waiting a respectable period of time for a presumption of death to seem warranted. Ideally, all that we required was the cooperation of one person. Either Caine or Julian—it did not matter which. You see, Bleys had already gone off into Shadow and was in the process of putting together a large military force—"

"Bleys! He was one of you?"

"Indeed. We intended him for the throne—with sufficient strings on him, of course, so that it would have amounted to a *de facto* triumvirate. So, he went off to assemble troops, as I was saying. We hoped for a bloodless takeover, but we had to be ready in the event that words proved insufficient to win our case. If Julian gave us the land route in, or Caine the waves, we could have transported the troops with dispatch and held the day by force of arms, should that have proven necessary. Unfortunately, I chose the wrong man. In my estimate, Caine was Julian's superior in matters of corruption. So, with measured delicacy I sounded him on the matter. He seemed willing to go along with things, at first. But he either reconsidered subsequently or deceived me quite skillfully from the beginning. Naturally, I prefer to believe that it was the former. Whatever, at some point he came to the conclusion that he stood to benefit more by supporting a rival claimant. To wit, Eric. Now Eric's hopes had been somewhat dashed by Dad's attitude toward him—but Dad was gone, and our intended move gave Eric the chance to act as defender of the throne. Unfortunately for us, such a position would also put him but a step away from the throne itself. To make matters darker, Julian went along with Caine in pledging the loyalty of his troops to Eric, as defender. Thus was the other trio formed. So Eric took a public oath to defend the throne, and the lines were thereby drawn. I was naturally in a somewhat embarrassing position at this time. I bore the brunt of their animosity, as they did not know who my fellows were. Yet they could not imprison or torture me, for I would immediately be trumped out of their hands. And if they were to kill me, they realized there might well be a reprisal by parties unknown. So it had to stand as a stalemate for a time. They also saw that I could no longer move directly against them. They kept me under heavy surveillance. So a more devious route was charted. Again I disagreed and again I lost, two to one. We were to employ the same forces we had called upon to deal with Dad, this time for purposes of discrediting Eric. If the job of defending Amber, so confidently assumed, were to prove too much for him and Bleys then came onto the scene and handled the situation with dispatch, why Bleys would even have popular support as he moved on to assume the role of defender himself and—after a fit period of time—suffered the thrusting of sovereignty upon him, for the good of Amber."

"Question," I interrupted. "What about Benedict? I

know he was off being discontent in his Avalon, but if something really threatened Amber . . ."

"Yes," he said, nodding, "and for that reason, a part of our deal was to involve Benedict with a number of problems of his own."

I thought of the harassment of Benedict's Avalon by the hellmaids. I thought of the stump of his right arm. I opened my mouth to speak again, but Brand raised his hand.

"Let me finish in my own fashion, Corwin. I am not unmindful of your thought processes as you speak. I feel the pain in your side, twin to my own. Yes, I know these things and many more." His eyes burned strangely as he took another cigarette into his hand and it lit of its own accord. He drew heavily upon it and spoke as he exhaled. "I broke with the others over this decision. I saw it as involving too great a peril, as placing Amber herself in jeopardy. Broke with them . . ." He watched the smoke for several moments before he continued. "But things were too far advanced that I might simply walk away. I had to oppose them, in order to defend myself as well as Amber. It was too late to swing over to Eric's side. He would not have protected me if he could have—and besides, I was certain he was going to lose. It was then that I decided to employ certain new abilities I had acquired. I had often wondered at the strange relationship between Eric and Flora, off on that shadow Earth she pretended so to enjoy. I had had a slight suspicion that there was something about that place which concerned him, and that she might be his agent there. While I could not get close enough to him to achieve any satisfaction on this count, I felt confident that it would not take too much in the way of investigation, direct and otherwise, to learn what Flora was about. And so I did. Then suddenly the pace accelerated. My own party was concerned as to my whereabouts. Then when I picked you up and shocked back a few memories, Eric learned from Flora that something was suddenly quite amiss. Consequently, both sides were soon looking for me. I had decided that your return would throw everyone's plans out the window and get me out of the pocket I was in long enough to come up with an alternative to the way things were going. Eric's claim would be clouded once again, you would have had supporters of your own, my party would have lost the purpose for its entire maneuver and I had assumed you would not be ungrateful to me for my part in things. Then you went and escaped from Porter, and things really got complicated. All of us were looking for you, as I later learned, for different reasons. But my former associates had something very extra going for them. They learned what was happening, located you, and got there first. Obviously, there was a very simple way to preserve the status quo, where they would continue to hold the edge. Bleys fired the shots that put you and your car into the lake. I arrived just as this was occurring. He departed almost immediately, for it looked as if he had done a thorough job. I dragged you out, though, and there was enough left to start treating. It was frustrating now that I think back on it, not knowing whether the treatment had really been effective, whether you would awaken as Corwin or Corey. It was frustrating afterward, also, still not knowing. . . . I hellrode out when help arrived. My associates caught up with me somewhat later and put me where you found me. Do you know the rest of the story?"

"Not all of it."

"Then stop me whenever we've caught up on this. I only obtained it later, myself. Eric's crowd learned of the accident, got your location, and had you transferred to a private place, where you could be better protected, and kept you heavily sedated, so that *they* could be protected."

"Why should Eric protect me, especially if my presence was going to wreck his plans?"

"By then, seven of us knew you were still living.

That was too many. It was simply too late to do what he would have liked to do. He was still trying to live down Dad's words. If anything had happened to you once you were in his power, it would have blocked his movement to the throne. If Benedict ever got word of it, or Gérard . . . No, he'd not have made it. Afterward, yes. Before, no. What happened was that general knowledge of the fact of your existence forced his hand. He scheduled his coronation and resolved to keep you out of the way until it had occurred. An extremely premature bit of business, not that I see he had much of a choice. I guess you know what happened after that, since it happened to you."

"I fell in with Bleys, just as he was making his move. Not too fortunate."

He shrugged.

"Oh, it might have been—if you had won, and if you had been able to do something about Bleys. You hadn't a chance, though, not really. My grasp of their motivations begins to dissolve at this point, but I believe that that entire assault really constituted some sort of feint."

"Why?"

"As I said, I do not know. But they already had Eric just about where they wanted him. It should not have been necessary to call that attack."

I shook my head. Too much, too fast . . . Many of the facts sounded true, once I subtracted the narrator's bias. But still . . .

"I don't know . . ." I began.

"Of course," he said. "But if you ask me I will tell you."

"Who was the third member of your group?"

"The same person who stabbed me, of course. Would you care to venture a guess?"

"Just tell me."

"Fiona. The whole thing was her idea."

"Why didn't you tell me that right away?"

"Because you would not have sat still long enough to hear the rest of what I had to say. You would have dashed off to put her under restraint, discovered that she was gone, roused all the others, started an investigation, and wasted a lot of valuable time. You still may, but it at least provided me with your attention for a sufficient time for me to convince you that I know what I am about. Now, when I tell you that time is essential and that you must hear the rest of what I have to say as soon as possible—if Amber is to have any chance at all—you might listen rather than chase a crazy lady."

I had already half risen from my chair.

"I shouldn't go after her?" I said.

"The hell with her, for now. You've got bigger problems. You had better sit down again."

So I did.

10

A raft of moonbeams . . . the ghostly torchlight, like fires in black-and-white films . . . stars . . . a few fine filaments of mist . . .

I leaned upon the rail, I looked across the world. . . . Utter silence held the night, the dream-drenched city, the entire universe from here. Distant things—the sea, Amber, Arden, Garnath, the Lighthouse of Cabra, the Grove of the Unicorn, my tomb atop Kolvir . . . Silent, far below, yet clear, distinct . . . A god's eye view, I'd say, or that of a soul cut loose and drifting high . . . In the middle of the night . . .

I had come to the place where the ghosts play at being ghosts, where the omens, portents, signs, and animate desires thread the nightly avenues and palace high halls of Amber in the sky, Tir-na Nog'th . . .

Turning, my back to the rail and dayworld's vestiges below, I regarded the avenues and dark terraces, the halls of the lords, the quarters of the low. . . . The moonlight is intense in Tir-na Nog'th, silvers over the facing sides of all our imaged places. . . . Stick in hand, I passed forward, and the strangelings moved about me, appeared at windows, on balconies, on benches, at gates . . . Unseen I passed, for truly put, in this place I was the ghost to whatever their substance. . . .

Silence and silver . . . Only the tapping of my stick, and that mostly muted . . . More mists adrift toward the heart of things . . . The palace a white bonfire of it . . . Dew, like drops of mercury on the finely sanded petals and stems in the gardens by the walks . . . The passing moon as painful to the eye as the sun at midday, the stars outshone, dimmed by it . . . Silver and silence . . . The shine . . .

I had not planned on coming, for its omens—if that they truly be—are deceitful, its similarities to the lives and places below unsettling, its spectacle often disconcerting. Still, I had come. . . . A part of my bargain with time . . .

After I had left Brand to continue his recovery in the keeping of Gérard, I had realized that I required additional rest myself and sought to obtain it without betraying my disability. Fiona was indeed flown, and neither she nor Julian could be reached by means of the Trumps. Had I told Benedict and Gérard what Brand had told me, I was certain that they would have insisted we begin efforts at tracking her down, at tracking both of them. I was equally certain that such efforts would prove useless.

I had sent for Random and Ganelon and retired to my quarters, giving out that I intended to pass the day in rest and quiet thought in anticipation of spending the night in Tir-na Nog'th—reasonable behavior for any Amberite with a serious problem. I did not put much stock in the practice, but most of the others did. As it was the perfect time for me to be about such a thing, I felt that it would make my day's retirement believable. Of course, this obliged me to follow through on it that night. But this, too, was good. It gave me a day, a night, and part of the following day in which to heal sufficiently to carry my wound that much the better. I felt that it would be time well spent.

You've got to tell someone, though. I told Random and I told Ganelon. Propped in my bed, I told them of the plans of Brand, Fiona, and Bleys, and of the Eric-Julian-Caine cabal. I told them what Brand had said concerning my return and his own imprisonment by his fellow conspirators. They saw why the survivors of both factions—Fiona and Julian—had run off: doubtless to marshal their forces, hopefully to expend them on one another, but probably not. Not immediately, anyhow. More likely, one or the other would move to take Amber first.

"They will just have to take numbers and wait their turns, like everyone else," Random had said.

"Not exactly," I remembered saying. "Fiona's allies and the things that have been coming in on the black road are the same guys."

"And the Circle in Lorraine?" Ganelon had asked.

"The same. That was how it manifested itself in that shadow. They came a great distance."

"Ubiquitous bastards," Random had said.

Nodding, I had tried to explain.

. . . And so I came to Tir-na Nog'th. When the moon rose and the apparition of Amber came faintly into the heavens, stars showing through it, pale halo about its towers, tiny flecks of movement upon its walls, I waited, waited with Ganelon and Random, waited on the highest crop of Kolvir, there where the three steps are fashioned, roughly, out of the stone. . . .

When the moonlight touched them, the outline of the entire stairway began to take shape, spanning the great gulf to that point above the sea the vision city held. When the moonlight fell full upon it, the stair had taken as much of substance as it would ever possess, and I set my foot on the stone. . . . Random held a full deck of Trumps and I'd mine within my jacket. Grayswandir, forged upon this very stone by moonlight, held power in the city in the sky, and so I bore my blade along. I had rested all day, and I held a staff to lean upon. Illusion of distance and time . . . The stairs through the Corwin-ignoring sky escalate somehow, for it is not a simple arithmetic progression up them once motion has commenced. I was here, I was there, I was a quarter of the way up before my shoulder had forgotten the clasp of Ganelon's hand. . . . If I looked too hard at any portion of the stair, it lost its shimmering opacity and I saw the ocean far below as through a translucent lens. . . . I lost track of time, though it

seems it's never long, afterward . . . As far beneath the
waves as I'd soon be above them, off to my right, glit-
tering and curling, the outline of Rebma appeared within
the sea. I thought of Moire, wondered how she fared.
What would become of our deepwater double should
Amber ever fall? Would the image remain unshattered
in its mirror? Or would building blocks and bones be
taken and shaken alike, dice in the deepwater casino
canyons our fleets fly over? No answer in the man-
drowning, Corwin-confounding waters, though I felt
a twinge in my side.

At the head of the stair, I entered, coming into the
ghost city as one would enter Amber after mounting
the great forestair up Kolvir's seaward face.

I leaned upon the rail, looked across the world.

The black road led off to the south. I could not see
it by night. Not that it mattered. I knew now where it
led. Or rather where Brand said that it led. As he
appeared to have used up a life's worth of reasons for
lying, I believed that I knew where it led.

All the way.

From the brightness of Amber and the power and
clean-shining splendor of adjacent Shadow, off through
the progressively darkening slices of image that lead
away in any direction, farther, through the twisted land-
scapes, and farther still, on through places seen only
when drunk, delirious, or dreamingly illy, and farther
yet again, running beyond the place where I stop. . . .
Where *I* stop . . .

How to put simply that which is not a simple
thing . . . ? Solipsism, I suppose, is where we have to
begin—the notion that nothing exists but the self, or,
at least, that we cannot truly be aware of anything but
our own existence and experience. I can find, somewhere, off in Shadow, anything I can visualize. Any of us
can. This, in good faith, does not transcend the limits
of the ego. It may be argued, and in fact has, by most
of us, that we create the shadows we visit out of the
stuff of our own psyches, that we alone truly exist, that

the shadows we traverse are but projections of our own desires. . . . Whatever the merits of this argument, and there are several, it does go far toward explaining much of the family's attitude toward people, places, and things outside of Amber. Namely, we are toymakers and they, our playthings—sometimes dangerously animated, to be sure; but this, too, is part of the game. We are impresarios by temperament, and we treat one another accordingly. While solipsism does tend to leave one slightly embarrassed on questions of etiology, one can easily avoid the embarrassment by refusing to admit the validity of the questions. Most of us are, as I have often observed, almost entirely pragmatic in the conduct of our affairs. Almost . . .

Yet—yet there is a disturbing element in the picture. There is a place where the shadows go mad. . . . When you purposely push yourself through layer after layer of Shadow, surrendering—again, purposely—a piece of your understanding every step of the way, you come at last to a mad place beyond which you cannot go. Why do this? In hope of an insight, I'd say, or a new game . . . But when you come to this place, as we all have, you realize that you have reached the limit of Shadow or the end of yourself—synonymous terms, as we had always thought. Now, though . . .

Now I know that it is not so, now as I stand, waiting, without the Courts of Chaos, telling you what it was like, I know that it is not so. But I knew well enough then, that night, in Tir-na Nog'th, had known earlier, when I had fought the goat-man in the Black Circle of Lorraine, had known that day in the Lighthouse of Cabra, after my escape from the dungeons of Amber, when I had looked upon ruined Garnath. . . . I knew that that was not all there was to it. I knew because I knew that the black road ran beyond that point. It passed through madness into chaos and kept going. The things that traveled across it came from somewhere, but they were not my things. I had somehow helped to grant them this passage, but they did not spring from

my version of reality. They were their own, or someone else's—small matter there—and they tore holes in
that small metaphysic we had woven over the ages.
They had entered our preserve, they were not of it, they
threatened it, they threatened us. Fiona and Brand had
reached beyond everything and found something, where
none of the rest of us had believed anything to exist.
The danger released was, on some level, almost worth
the evidence obtained: we were not alone, nor were
shadows truly our toys. Whatever our relationship with
Shadow, I could nevermore regard it in the old light. . . .

All because the black road headed south and ran
beyond the end of the world, where I stop.

Silence and silver . . . Walking away from the rail,
leaning on my stick, passing through the fog-spun, mist-
woven, moonlight-brushed fabric of vision within the
troubling city . . . Ghosts . . . Shadows of shadows . . .
Images of probability . . . Might-bes and might-have-
beens . . . Probability lost . . . Probability regained . . .

Walking, across the promenade now . . . Figures,
faces, many of them familiar . . . What are they about?
Hard to say . . . Some lips move, some faces show
animation. There are no words there for me. I pass
among them, unnoted.

There . . . One such figure . . . Alone, but waiting . . .
Fingers unknotting minutes, casting them away . . . Face
averted, and I wish to see it . . . A sign that I will or
should . . . She sits on a stone bench beneath a gnarly
tree . . . She gazes in the direction of the palace . . .
Her form is quite familiar . . . Approaching, I see that
it is Lorraine . . . She continues to regard a point far
beyond me, does not hear me say that I have avenged
her death.

But mine is the power to be heard here. . . . It hangs
in the sheath at my side.

Drawing Grayswandir, I raise my blade overhead
where moonlight tricks its patterns into a kind of motion. I place it on the ground between us.

"Corwin!"

Her head snaps back, her hair rusts in the moonlight, her eyes focus.

"Where did you come from? You're early."

"You wait for me?"

"Of course. You told me to—"

"How did you come to this place?"

"This bench . . . ?"

"No. This city."

"Amber? I do not understand. You brought me yourself. I—"

"Are you happy here?"

"You know that I am, so long as I am with you."

I had not forgotten the evenness of her teeth, the hint of freckles beneath the soft light's veil. . . .

"What happened? It is very important. Pretend for a moment that I do not know, and tell me everything that happened to us after the battle of the Black Circle in Lorraine."

She frowned. She stood. She turned away.

"We had that argument," she said. "You followed me, drove away Melkin, and we talked. I saw that I was wrong and I went with you to Avalon. There, your brother Benedict persuaded you to talk with Eric. You were not reconciled, but you agreed to a truce because of something that he told you. He swore not to harm you and you swore to defend Amber, with Benedict to witness both oaths. We remained in Avalon while you obtained chemicals, and we went to another place later, a place where you purchased strange weapons. We won the battle, but Eric lies wounded now." She stood and faced me. "Are you thinking of ending the truce? Is that it, Corwin?"

I shook my head, and though I knew better I reached to embrace her. I wanted to hold her, despite the fact that one of us did not exist, could not exist, when that tiny gap of space between our skins was crossed, to tell her that whatever had happened or would happen—

The shock was not severe, but it caused me to stum-

ble. I lay across Grayswandir. . . . My staff had fallen
to the grass several paces away. Rising to my knees, I
saw that the color had gone out of her face, her eyes,
her hair. Her mouth shaped ghost words as her head
turned, searching. Sheathing Grayswandir, recovering
my staff, I rose once again. Her seeing passed through
me and focused. Her face grew smooth, she smiled,
started forward. I moved aside and turned, watching
her run toward the man who approached, seeing her
clasped in his arms, glimpsing his face as he bent it
toward her own, lucky ghost, silver rose at the throat
of his garment, kissing her, this man I would never
know, silver on silence, and silver. . . .

Walking away . . . Not looking back . . . Crossing the
promenade . . .

The voice of Random: "Corwin, are you all right?"

"Yes."

"Anything interesting happening?"

"Later, Random."

"Sorry."

And sudden, the gleaming stair before the palace
grounds . . . Up it, and a turn to the right . . . Slow
and easy now, into the garden . . . Ghost flowers
throb on their stalks all about me, ghost shrubs spill
blossoms like frozen firework displays. *Sans* colors,
all . . . Only the essentials sketched in, degrees of
luminosity in silver the terms of their claim on the eye.
Only the essentials here. Is Tir-na Nog'th a special
sphere of Shadow in the real world, swayed by the
promptings of the id—a full-sized projective test in the
sky, perhaps even a therapeutic device? Despite the
silver, I'd say, if this is a piece of the soul, the night
is very dark. . . . And silent . . .

Walking . . . By fountains, benches, groves, cunning
alcoves in mazes of hedging . . . Passing along the walks,
up an occasional step, across small bridges . . . Moving past ponds, among trees, by an odd piece of statu-
ary, a boulder, a sundial (moondial, here?), bearing
to my right, pressing steadily ahead, rounding, after a

time, the northern end of the palace, swinging left
then, past a courtyard overhung by balconies, more
ghosts here and there upon them, behind them, within . . .

Circling around to the rear, just to see the back
gardens this way, again, for they are lovely by normal
moonlight in the true Amber.

A few more figures, talking, standing . . . No motion but my own is apparent.

. . . And feel myself drawn to the right. As one
should never turn down a free oracle, I go.

. . . Toward a mass of high hedging, a small open area
within, if it is not overgrown . . . Long ago there was . . .

Two figures, embracing, within. They part as I begin
to turn away. None of my affair, but . . . Deirdre . . .
One of them is Deirdre. I know who the man will be
before he turns. It is a cruel joke by whatever powers
rule that silver, that silence. . . . Back, back, away from
that hedge . . . Turning, stumbling, rising again, going,
away, now, quickly . . .

The voice of Random: "Corwin? Are you all right?"

"Later! Damn it! Later!"

"It is not too long till sunrise, Corwin. I felt I had
better remind you—"

"Consider me reminded!"

Away, now, quickly . . . Time, too, is a dream in
Tir-na Nog'th. Small comfort, but better than none.
Quickly, now, away, going, again . . .

. . . Toward the palace, bright architecture of the
mind or spirit, more clearly standing now than the
real ever did . . . To judge perfection is to render a
worthless verdict, but I must see what lies within. . . .
This must be an end of sorts, for I am driven. I had
not paused to recover my staff from where it had
fallen this time, among the sparkling grasses. I know
where I must go, what I must do. Obvious now, though
the logic which has seized me is not that of the waking mind.

Hurrying, climbing, up to the rearward portal . . .

The side-biting soreness comes home again . . . Across the threshold, in . . .

Into an absence of starshine and moonlight. The illumination is without direction, seeming almost to drift and to pool, aimlessly. Wherever it misses, the shadows are absolute, occulting large sections of room, hallway, closet, and stair.

Among them, through them, almost running now . . . Monochrome of my home . . . Apprehension overtakes me . . . The black spots seem like holes in this piece of reality now. . . . I fear to pass too near. Fall in and be lost . . .

Turning . . . Crossing . . . Finally . . . Entering . . . The throne room . . . Bushels of blackness stacked where my eyes would drive down lines of seeing to the throne itself . . .

There, though, is movement.

A drifting, to my right, as I advance.

A lifting, with the drifting.

The boots on feet on legs come into view as forward pressing I near the place's base.

Grayswandir comes into my hand, finding its way into a patch of light, renewing its eyetricking, shape-shifting stretch, acquiring a glow of its own . . .

I place my left foot on the step, rest my left hand on my knee. Distracting but bearable, the throb of my healing gut. I wait for the blackness, the emptiness, to be drawn, appropriate curtain for the theatrics with which I am burdened this night.

And it slides aside, revealing a hand, an arm, a shoulder, the arm a glinting, metallic thing, its planes like the facets of a gem, its wrist and elbow wondrous weaves of silver cable, pinned with flecks of fire, the hand, stylized, skeletal, a Swiss toy, a mechanical insect, functional, deadly, beautiful in its way . . .

And it slides aside, revealing the rest of the man. . . .

Benedict stands relaxed beside the throne, his left and human hand laid lightly upon it. He leans toward the throne. His lips are moving.

And it slides aside, revealing the throne's occupant. . . .

"Dara!"

Turned toward her right, she smiles, she nods to Benedict, her lips move. I advance and extend Grayswandir till its point rests lightly in the concavity beneath her sternum . . . .

Slowly, quite slowly, she turns her head and meets my eyes. She takes on color and life. Her lips move again, and this time her words reach me.

"What are you?"

"No. That is my question. You answer it. Now."

"I am Dara. Dara of Amber, Queen Dara. I hold this throne by right of blood and conquest. Who are you?"

"Corwin. Also of Amber. Don't move! I did not ask *who* you are—"

"Corwin is dead these many centuries. I have seen his tomb."

"Empty."

"Not so. His body lies within."

"Give me your lineage!"

Her eyes move to her right, where the shade of Benedict still stands. A blade has appeared in his new hand, seeming almost an extension of it, but he holds it loosely, casually. His left hand now rests on her arm. His eyes seek me in back of Grayswandir's hilt. Failing, they go again to that which is visible—Grayswandir—recognizing its design. . . .

"I am the great-granddaughter of Benedict and the hellmaid Lintra, whom he loved and later slew." Benedict winces at this, but she continues. "I never knew her. My mother and my mother's mother were born in a place where time does not run as in Amber. I am the first of my mother's line to bear all the marks of humanity. And you, Lord Corwin, are but a ghost from a long dead past, albeit a dangerous shade. How you came here, I do not know. But it was wrong of you. Return to your grave. Trouble not the living."

My hand wavers. Grayswandir strays no more than half an inch. Yet that is sufficient.

Benedict's thrust is below my threshold of perception. His new arm drives the new hand that holds the blade that strikes Grayswandir, as his old arm draws his old hand, which has seized upon Dara, back across the arm of the throne. . . . This subliminal impression reaches me moments later, as I fall back, cutting air, recover and strike an *en garde,* reflexively. . . . It is ridiculous for a pair of ghosts to fight. Here, it is uneven. He cannot even reach me, whereas Grayswandir—

But no! His blade changes hands as he releases Dara and pivots, bringing them together, old hand and new. His left wrist rotates as he slides it forward and down, moving into what would be *corps à corps,* were we two facing mortal bodies. For a moment our guards are locked. That moment is enough. . . .

That gleaming, mechanical hand comes forward, a thing of moonlight and fire, blackness and smoothness, all angles, no curves, fingers slightly flexed, palm silver-scribbled with a half-familiar design, comes forward, comes forward and catches at my throat. . . .

Missing, the fingers catch my shoulder and the thumb goes hooking—whether for clavicle or larynx, I do not know. I throw one punch with my left, toward his midsection, and there is nothing there. . . .

The voice of Random: "Corwin! The sun is about to rise! You've got to come down now!"

I cannot even answer. A second or two and that hand would tear away whatever it held. That hand . . . Grayswandir and that hand, which strangely resembles it, are the only two things which seem to coexist in my world and the city of ghosts. . . .

"I see it, Corwin! Pull away and reach for me! The Trump—"

I spin Grayswandir out of the bind and bring it around and down in a long, slashing arc. . . .

Only a ghost could have beaten Benedict or Benedict's ghost with that maneuver. We stand too close for

him to block my blade, but his countercut, perfectly
placed, would have removed my arm, had there been
an arm there to meet it. . . .

As there is not, I complete the stroke, delivering the
blow with the full force of my right arm, high upon
that lethal device of moonlight and fire, blackness and
smoothness, near to the point where it is joined with
him.

With an evil tearing at my shoulder, the arm comes
away from Benedict and grows still. . . . We both fall.

"Get up! By the unicorn, Corwin, get up! The sun
is rising! The city will come apart about you!"

The floor beneath me wavers to and from a misty
transparency. I glimpse a light-scaled expanse of water.
I roll to my feet, barely avoiding the ghost's rush to
clutch at the arm he has lost. It clings like a dead
parasite and my side is hurting again. . . .

Suddenly I am heavy and the vision of ocean does
not fade. I begin to sink through the floor. Color returns
to the world, wavering stripes of pink. The Corwin-
spurning floor parts and the Corwin-killing gulf is
opened. . . .

I fall. . . .

"This way, Corwin! Now!"

Random stands on a mountaintop and reaches for
me. I extend my hand. . . .

. . . And frying pans without fires are often far between . . .

We untangled ourselves and rose. I sat down again
immediately, on the bottommost stair. I worked the
metal hand loose from my shoulder—no blood there,
but a promise of bruises to come—then cast it and
its arm to the ground. The light of early morning did
not detract from its exquisite and menacing appearance.

Ganelon and Random stood beside me.

"You all right, Corwin?"

"Yes. Just let me catch my breath."

"I brought food," Random said. "We could have
breakfast right here."

"Good idea."

As Random began unpacking provisions, Ganelon
nudged the arm with the toe of his boot.

"What the hell," he asked, "is that?"

I shook my head.

"I lopped it off the ghost of Benedict," I told him.
"For reasons I do not understand, it was able to reach
me."

He stooped and picked it up, studied it.

"A lot lighter than I thought it would be," he observed. He raked the air with it. "You could do quite
a job on someone, with a hand like that."

"I know."

He worked the fingers.

"Maybe the real Benedict could use it."

"Maybe," I said. "My feelings are quite mixed when it comes to offering it to him, but possibly you're right. . . ."

"How's the side?"

I prodded it gently.

"Not especially bad, everything considered. I'll be able to ride after breakfast, so long as we take it nice and easy."

"Good. Say, Corwin, while Random is getting things ready, I have a question that may be out of order, but it has been bothering me all along."

"Ask it."

"Well, let me put it this way: I am all for you, or I would not be here. I will fight for you to have your throne, no matter what. But every time talk of the succession occurs, someone gets angry and breaks it off or the subject gets changed. Like Random did, while you were up there. I suppose that it is not absolutely essential for me to know the basis of your claim to the throne, or that of any of the others, but I cannot help being curious as to the reasons for all the friction."

I sighed, then sat silent for a time.

"All right," I said after a while, and then I chuckled. "All right. If we cannot agree on these things ourselves, I would guess that they must seem pretty confused to an outsider. Benedict is the eldest. His mother was Cymnea. She bore Dad two other sons, also— Osric and Finndo. Then—how does one put these things?—Faiella bore Eric. After that, Dad found some defect in his marriage with Cymnea and had it dissolved—*ab initio,* as they would say in my old shadow —from the beginning. Neat trick, that. But he was the king."

"Didn't that make all of them illegitimate?"

"Well, it left their status less certain. Osric and Finndo were more than a little irritated, as I understand it, but they died shortly thereafter. Benedict was either less irritated or more politic about the entire affair. He never raised a fuss. Dad then married Faiella."

"And that made Eric legitimate?"

"It would have, if he had acknowledged Eric as his son. He treated him as if he were, but he never did anything formal in that regard. It involved the smoothing-over process with Cymnea's family, which had become a bit stronger around that time."

"Still, if he treated him as his own . . ."

"Ah! But he later *did* acknowledge Llewella formally. She was born out of wedlock, but he decided to recognize her, poor girl. All of Eric's supporters hated her for its effect on his status. Anyway, Faiella was later to become my mother. I was born safely in wedlock, making me the first with a clean claim on the throne. Talk to one of the others and you may get a different line of reasoning, but those are the facts it will have to be based on. Somehow it does not seem quite as important as it once did, though, with Eric dead and Benedict not really interested. . . . But that is where I stand."

"I see—sort of," he said. "Just one more thing, then . . ."

"What?"

"Who is next? That is to say, if anything were to happen to you . . . ?"

I shook my head.

"It gets even more complicated there, now. Caine would have been next. With him dead, I see it as swinging over to Clarissa's brood—the redheads. Bleys would have followed, then Brand."

"Clarissa? What became of your mother?"

"She died in childbirth. Deirdre was the child. Dad did not remarry for many years after mother's death. When he did, it was a redheaded wench from a far southern shadow. I never liked her. He began feeling the same way after a time and started fooling around again. They had one reconciliation after Llewella's birth in Rebma, and Brand was the result. When they were finally divorced, he recognized Llewella to spite Clarissa. At least, that is what I think happened."

"So you are not counting the ladies in the succession?"

"No. They are neither interested nor fit. If I were, though, Fiona would precede Bleys and Llewella would follow him. After Clarissa's crowd, it would swing over to Julian, Gérard, and Random, in that order. Excuse me—count Flora before Julian. The marriage data is even more involved, but no one will dispute the final order. Let it go at that."

"Gladly," he said. "So now Brand gets it if you die, right?"

"Well . . . He is a self-confessed traitor and he rubs everybody the wrong way. I do not believe the rest of them would have him, as he stands now. But I do not believe he has by any means given up."

"But the alternative is Julian."

I shrugged.

"The fact that I do not like Julian does not make him unfit. In fact, he might even be a very effective monarch."

"So he knifed you for the chance to prove it," Random called out. "Come on and eat."

"I still don't think so," I said, getting to my feet and heading for the food. "First, I don't see how he could have gotten to me. Second, it would have been too damned obvious. Third, if I die in the near future Benedict will have the real say as to the succession. Everyone knows that. He's got the seniority, he's got the wits, and he's got the power. He could simply say, for example, 'The hell with all this bickering, I am backing Gérard,' and that would be it."

"What if he decided to reinterpret his own status and take it himself?" Ganelon asked.

We seated ourselves on the ground and took the tin dishes Random had filled.

"He could have had it long before this, had he wanted it," I said. "There are several ways of regarding the offspring of a void marriage, and the most favorable one would be the most likely in his case. Osric and

Finndo rushed to judgment, taking the worst view. Benedict knew better. He just waited. So . . . It is possible. Unlikely, though, I'd say."

"Then—in the normal course of affairs—if anything happened to you, it could still be very much in the air?"

"Very much."

"But why was Caine killed?" Random asked. Then, between mouthfuls, he answered his own question. "So that when they got you, it would swing over to Clarissa's kids immediately. It has occurred to me that Bleys is probably still living, and he is next in line. His body was never found. My guess is this: He trumped off to Fiona during your attack and returned to Shadow to rebuild his forces, leaving you to what he hoped would be your death at the hands of Eric. He is finally ready to move again. So they killed Caine and tried for you. If they are really allied with the black-road horde, they could have arranged for another assault from that quarter. Then he could have done the same thing you did—arrive at the last hour, turn back the invaders, and move on in. And there he would be, next in line and first in force. Simple. Except that you survived and Brand has been returned. If we are to believe Brand's accusation of Fiona—and I see no reason why we should not—then it follows from their original program."

I nodded.

"Possibly," I said. "I asked Brand just those things. He admitted their possibility, but he disavowed any knowledge as to whether Bleys was still living. Personally, I think he was lying."

"Why?"

"It is possible that he wishes to combine revenge for his imprisonment and the attempt on his life with the removal of the one impediment, save for myself, to his own succession. I think he feels that I will be expended in a scheme he is evolving to deal with the black road. The destruction of his own cabal and the removal of the road could make him look pretty decent,

especially after all the penance he has had thrust upon
him. Then, maybe then, he would have a chance—or
thinks that he would."

"Then you think Bleys is still living, too?"

"Just a feeling," I said. "But yes, I do."

"What is their strength, anyway?"

"An endorsement of higher education," I said. "Fiona
and Brand paid attention to Dworkin while the rest of
us were off indulging our assorted passions in Shadow.
Consequently, they seem to have obtained a better grasp
of principles than we possess. They know more about
Shadow and what lies beyond it, more about the Pattern, more about the Trumps than we do. That is why
Brand was able to send you his message."

"An interesting thought . . ." Random mused. "Do
you think they might have disposed of Dworkin after
they felt they had learned enough from him? It would
certainly help to keep things exclusive, if anything happened to Dad."

"That thought had not occurred to me," I said.

And I wondered, could they have done something
that had affected his mind? Something that left him
as he was when last I had seen him? If so, were they
aware that he was possibly still living, somewhere? Or
might they have assumed his total destruction?

"Yes, an interesting thought," I said. "I suppose
that it is possible."

The sun inched its way upward, and the food restored me. No trace of Tir-na Nog'th remained in the
morning's light. My memories of it had already taken
on the quality of images in a dim mirror. Ganelon
fetched its only other token, the arm, and Random
packed it away along with the dishes. By daylight, the
first three steps looked less like stairs and more like
jumbled rock.

Random gestured with his head.

"Take the same way back?" he asked.

"Yes," I said, and we mounted.

We had come by way of a trail that wound about

Kolvir to the south. It was longer but less rugged than the route across the crest. I'd a humor to pamper myself so long as my side protested.

So we bore to the right, moving single file, Random in the lead, Ganelon to the rear. The trail ran gently upward, then cut back down again. The air was cool, and it bore the aromas of verdure and moist earth, a thing quite unusual in that stark place, at that altitude. Straying air currents, I reasoned, from the forest far below.

We let the horses pick their own casual pace down through the dip and up the next rise. As we neared its crest, Random's horse whinnied and began to rear. He controlled it immediately, and I glanced about but saw nothing that might have startled it.

When he reached its summit, Random slowed and called back, "Take a look at that sunrise now, will you?"

It would have been rather difficult to avoid doing so, though I did not remark on the fact. Random was seldom given to sentimentality over vegetation, geology, or illumination.

I almost drew rein myself as I topped the rise, for the sun was a fantastic golden ball. It seemed half again its normal size, and its peculiar coloration was unlike anything I remembered having seen before. It did marvelous things to the band of ocean that had come into view above the next rise, and the tints of cloud and sky were indeed singular. I did not halt, though, for the sudden brightness was almost painful.

"You're right," I called out, following him down into the next declivity. Behind me, Ganelon snorted an appreciative oath.

When I had blinked away the aftereffects of that display I noticed that the vegetation was heavier than I had remembered in this little pocket in the sky. I had thought there were several scrubby trees and some patches of lichen, but there were actually several dozen trees, larger than I recalled, and greener, with a clutch of grasses here and there and a vine or two softening the outlines of the rocks. However, since my return I had only passed this way after dark. And now that I thought of it, it was probably the source of the aromas that had come to me earlier.

Passing through, it seemed that the little hollow was also wider than I recalled it. By the time we had crossed and were ascending once more, I was certain of it.

"Random," I called out, "has this place changed recently?"

"Hard to say," he answered. "Eric didn't let me out much. It seems to have grown up a bit."

"It seems bigger—wider."

"Yes, it does. I had thought that that was just my imagination."

When we reached the next crest I was not dazzled again because the sun was blocked by foliage. The area ahead of us contained many more trees than the one we had just departed—and they were larger and closer together. We drew rein.

"I don't remember this," he said. "Even passing through at night, it would have registered. We must have taken a wrong turn."

"I don't see how. Still, we know about where we are. I would rather go ahead than go back and start again. We should keep aware of conditions around Amber, anyway."

"True."

He headed down toward the wood. We followed.

"It's kind of unusual, at this altitude—a growth like this," he called back.

"There also seems to be a lot more soil than I recall."

"I believe you are right."

The trail curved to the left as we entered among the trees. I could see no reason for this deviation from the direct route. We stayed with it, however, and it added to the illusion of distance. After a few moments it swung suddenly to the right again. The prospect on cutting back was peculiar. The trees seemed even taller and were now so dense as to puzzle the eye that sought their penetration. When it turned once more it broadened, and the way was straight for a great distance ahead. Too great, in fact. Our little dell just wasn't that wide.

Random halted again.

"Damn it, Corwin! This is ridiculous!" he said. "You are not playing games, are you?"

"I couldn't if I would," I said. "I have never been able to manipulate Shadow anywhere on Kolvir. There isn't supposed to be any to work with here."

"That has always been my understanding, too. Amber casts Shadow but is not of it. I don't like this at all. What do you say we turn back?"

"I've a feeling we might not be able to retrace our way," I said. "There has to be a reason for this, and I want to know it."

"It occurs to me that it might be some sort of a trap."

"Even so," I said.

He nodded and we rode on, down that shaded way, under trees now grown more stately. The wood was silent about us. The ground remained level, the trail straight. Half consciously, we pushed the horses to a greater pace.

About five minutes passed before we spoke again. Then Random said, "Corwin, this can't be Shadow."

"Why not?"

"I have been trying to influence it and nothing happens. Have you tried?"

"No."

"Why don't you?"

"All right."

A rock could jut beyond the coming tree, a morning glory twine and bell within that shrubby stand. . . . There ought a patch of sky come clear, a wispy cloud upon it. . . . Then let there be a fallen limb, a stair of fungus up its side. . . . A scummed-over puddle . . . A frog . . . Falling feather, drifting seed . . . A limb that twists just so . . . Another trail upon our way, fresh-cut, deep-marked, past the place the feather should have fallen . . .

"No good," I said.

"If it is not Shadow, what is it?"

"Something else, of course."

He shook his head and checked again to see that his blade was loose in its scabbard. Automatically, I did the same. Moments later, I heard Ganelon's make a small clicking noise behind me.

Ahead, the trail began to narrow, and shortly thereafter it commenced to wander. We were forced to slow our pace once again, and the trees pressed nearer with branches sweeping lower than at any time before. The trail became a path. It jogged, it curved, it gave a final twist and then quit.

Random ducked a limb, then raised his hand and halted. We came up beside him. For as far as I could see ahead there was no indication of the trail's picking up again. Looking back, I failed to locate any sign of it either.

"Suggestions," he said, "are now in order. We do not know where we have been or where we are going, let alone where we are. My suggestion is the hell with curiosity. Let's get out of here the fastest way we know how."

"The Trumps?" Ganelon asked.

"Yes. What do you say, Corwin?"

"Okay. I don't like it either, and I can't think of anything better to try. Go ahead."

"Who should I try for?" he asked, producing his deck and uncasing it. "Gérard?"

"Yes."

He shuffled through his cards, located Gérard's, stared at it. We stared at him. Time went its way.

"I can't seem to reach him," he finally announced.

"Try Benedict."

"Okay."

Repeat performance. No contact.

"Try Deirdre," I said, drawing forth my own deck

and searching out her Trump. "I'll join you. We will see whether it makes a difference with two of us trying."

And again. And again.

"Nothing," I said after a long effort.

Random shook his head.

"Did you notice anything unusual about your Trumps?" he asked.

"Yes, but I don't know what it is. They do seem different."

"Mine seem to have lost that quality of coldness they once possessed," he said.

I shuffled mine slowly. I ran my fingertips across them.

"Yes, you are right," I said. "That's it. But let us try again. Say, Flora."

"Okay."

The results were the same. And with Llewella. And Brand.

"Any idea what could be wrong?" Random asked.

"Not the slightest. They couldn't all be blocking us. They couldn't all be dead. . . . Oh, I suppose they could. But it is highly unlikely. Something seems to have affected the Trumps themselves, is what it is. And I never knew of anything that could do that."

"Well, they are not guaranteed one hundred percent," Random said, "according to the manufacturer."

"What do you know that I don't?"

He chuckled.

"You never forget the day you come of age and walk the Pattern," he said. "I remember it as though it were last year. When I had succeeded—all flushed with excitement, with glory—Dworkin presented me with my first set of Trumps and instructed me in their use. I distinctly recall asking him whether they worked everywhere. And I remember his answer: 'No,' he said. 'But they should serve in any place you will ever be.' He never much liked me, you know."

"But did you ask him what he meant by that?"

"Yes, and he said, 'I doubt that you will ever achieve a state where they will fail to serve you. Why don't you run along now?' And I did. I was anxious to go play with the Trumps all by myself."

" 'Achieve a state?' He didn't say 'reach a place'?"

"No. I have a very good memory for certain things."

"Peculiar—though not much help that I can see. Smacks of the metaphysical."

"I'd wager Brand would know."

"I've a feeling you're right, for all the good that does us."

"We ought to do something other than discuss metaphysics," Ganelon commented. "If you can't manipulate Shadow and you can't work the Trumps, it would seem that the next thing to do is determine where we are. And then go looking for help."

I nodded.

"Since we are not in Amber, I think it is safe to assume that we are in Shadow—a very special place, quite near to Amber, since the changeover was not abrupt. In that we were transported without active cooperation on our part, there had to be some agency and presumably some intent behind the maneuver. If it is going to attack us, now is as good a time as any. If there is something else it wants, then it is going to have to show us, because we aren't even in a position to make a good guess."

"So you propose we do nothing?"

"I propose we wait. I don't see any value in wandering about, losing ourselves further."

"I seem to remember your once telling me that adjacent shadows tend to be somewhat congruent," Ganelon said.

"Yes, I probably did. So what?"

"Then, if we are as near to Amber as you suppose, we need but ride toward the rising sun to come to a spot that parallels the city itself."

"It is not quite that simple. But supposing it were, what good would it do us?"

"Perhaps the Trumps would function again at the point of maximum congruity."

Random looked at Ganelon, looked at me.

"That may be worth trying," he said. "What have we got to lose?"

"Whatever small orientation we still possess," I said. "Look, it is not a bad idea. If nothing develops here, we will try it. However, looking back, it seems that the road behind us closes in direct proportion to the distance we advance. We are not simply moving in space. Under these circumstances, I am loath to wander until I am satisfied that we have no other option. If someone desires our presence at a particular location, it is up to him now to phrase the invitation a little more legibly. We wait."

They both nodded. Random began to dismount, then froze, one foot in the stirrup, one on the ground.

"After all these years," he said, and, "I never really believed it . . ."

"What is it?" I whispered.

"The option," he said, and he mounted again.

He persuaded his horse to move very slowly forward. I followed, and a moment later I glimpsed it, white as I had seen it in the grove, standing, half hidden, amid a clump of ferns: the unicorn.

It turned as we moved, and seconds later flashed ahead, to stand partly concealed once more by the trunks of several trees.

"I see it!" Ganelon whispered. "To think there really is such a beast . . . Your family's emblem, isn't it?"

"Yes."

"A good sign, I'd say."

I did not answer, but followed, keeping it in sight. That it was meant to be followed I did not doubt.

It had a way of remaining partly concealed the entire while—looking out from behind something, passing from cover to cover, moving with an incredible swiftness when it did move, avoiding open areas, favoring glade and shade. We followed, deeper and deeper into

the wood which had given up all semblance of anything to be found on Kolvir's slopes. It resembled
Arden now, more than anything else near Amber, as
the ground was relatively level and the trees grew
more and more stately.

An hour had passed, I guessed, and another had followed it, before we came to a small, clear stream and
the unicorn turned and headed up it. As we rode along
the bank, Random commented, "This is starting to look
sort of familiar."

"Yes," I said, "but only sort of. I can't quite say
why."

"Nor I."

We entered upon a slope shortly thereafter, and it
grew steeper before very long. The going became more
difficult for the horses, but the unicorn adjusted its pace
to accommodate them. The ground became rockier, the
trees smaller. The stream curved in its splashing course.
I lost track of its twists and turns, but we were finally
nearing the top of the small mount up which we had
been traveling.

We achieved a level area and continued along it
toward the wood from which the stream issued. At this
point I caught an oblique view—ahead and to the right,
through a place where the land fell away—of an icy
blue sea, quite far below us.

"We're pretty high up," Ganelon said. "It seemed
like lowland, but—"

"The Grove of the Unicorn!" Random interrupted.
"That's what it looks like! See!"

Nor was he incorrect. Ahead lay an area strewn
with boulders. Amid them a spring uttered the stream
we followed. This place was larger and more lush, its
situation incorrect in terms of my internal compass.
Yet the similarity had to be more than coincidental.
The unicorn mounted the rock nearest the spring,
looked at us, then turned away. It might have been staring down at the ocean.

Then, as we continued, the grove, the unicorn, the

trees about us, the stream beside us took on an unusual clarity, all, as though each were radiating some special illumination, causing it to quiver with the intensity of its color while at the same time wavering, slightly, just at the edges of perception. This produced in me an incipient feeling like the beginning of the emotional accompaniment to a hellride.

Then, then and then, with each stride of my mount, something went out of the world about us. An adjustment in the relationships of objects suddenly occurred, eroding my sense of depth, destroying perspective, rearranging the display of articles within my field of vision, so that everything presented its entire outer surface without simultaneously appearing to occupy an increased area: angles predominated, and relative sizes seemed suddenly ridiculous. Random's horse reared and neighed, massive, apocalyptic, instantly recalling *Guernica* to my mind. And to my distress I saw that we ourselves had not been untouched by the phenomenon—but that Random, struggling with his mount, and Ganelon, still managing to control Firedrake, had, like everything else, been transfigured by this cubist dream of space.

But Star was a veteran of many a hellride; Firedrake, also, had been through a lot. We clung to them and felt the movements that we could not accurately gauge. And Random succeeded, at last, in imposing his will upon his mount, though the prospect continued to alter as we advanced.

Light values shifted next. The sky grew black, not as night, but like a flat, nonreflecting surface. So did certain vacant areas between objects. The only light left in the world seemed to originate from things themselves, and all of it was gradually bleached. Various intensities of white emerged from the planes of existence, and brightest of all, immense, awful, the unicorn suddenly reared, pawing at the air, filling perhaps ninety percent of creation with what became a slow-motion gesture I feared would annihilate us if we advanced another pace.

Then there was only the light.

Then absolute stillness.

Then the light was gone and there was nothing. Not even blackness. A gap in existence, which might have lasted an instant or an eternity . . .

Then the blackness returned, and the light. Only they were reversed. Light filled the interstices, outlining voids that must be objects. The first sound that I heard was the rushing of water, and I knew somehow that we were halted beside the spring. The first thing that I felt was Star's quivering. Then I smelled the sea.

Then the Pattern came into view, or a distorted negative of it. . . .

I leaned forward and more light leaked around the edges of things. I leaned back; it went away. Forward again, this time farther than before . . .

The light spread, introduced various shades of gray into the scheme of things. With my knees then, gently, I suggested that Star advance.

With each pace, something returned to the world. Surfaces, textures, colors . . .

Behind me, I heard the others begin to follow. Below me, the Pattern surrendered nothing of its mystery, but it acquired a context which, by degrees, found its place within the larger reshaping of the world about us.

Continuing downhill, a sense of depth reemerged. The sea, now plainly visible off to the right, underwent a possibly purely optical separation from the sky, with which it seemed momentarily to have been joined in some sort of *Urmeer* of the waters above and the waters below. Unsettling upon reflection, but unnoted while in effect. We were heading down a steep, rocky incline which seemed to have taken its beginning at the rear of the grove to which the unicorn had led us. Perhaps a hundred meters below us was a perfectly level area which appeared to be solid, unfractured rock—roughly oval in shape, a couple of hundred meters along its major axis. The slope down which we rode swung off to the left and returned, describing a vast arc, a parenthesis, half cupping the smooth shelf. Beyond its rightward jutting there was nothing—that is to say the land fell away in steep descent toward that peculiar sea.

And, continuing, all three dimensions seemed to reassert themselves once more. The sun was that great orb of molten gold we had seen earlier. The sky was a deeper blue than that of Amber, and there were no clouds in it. That sea was a matching blue, unspecked by sail or island. I saw no birds, and I heard no sounds other than our own. An enormous silence lay upon this place, this day. In the bowl of my suddenly clear vision, the Pattern at last achieved its disposition upon the surface below. I thought at first that it was inscribed in the rock, but as we drew nearer I saw that it was contained within it—gold-pink swirls, like veining in an exotic marble, natural-seeming despite the obvious purpose to the design.

I drew rein and the others came up beside me, Random to my right, Ganelon to my left.

We regarded it in silence for a long while. A dark, rough-edged smudge had obliterated an area of the section immediately beneath us, running from its outer rim to the center.

"You know," Random finally said, "it is as if someone had shaved the top off Kolvir, cutting at about the level of the dungeons."

"Yes," I said.

"Then—looking for congruence—that would be about where our own Pattern lies."

"Yes," I said again.

"And that blotted area is to the south, from whence comes the black road."

I nodded slowly as the understanding arrived and forged itself into a certainty.

"What does it mean?" he asked. "It seems to correspond to the true state of affairs, but beyond that I do not understand its significance. Why have we been brought here and shown this thing?"

"It does not correspond to the true state of affairs," I said. "It *is* the true state of affairs."

Ganelon turned toward us.

"On that shadow Earth we visited—where you had spent so many years—I heard a poem about two roads that diverged in a wood," he said. "It ends, 'I took the one less traveled by, and that has made all the difference.' When I heard it, I thought of something you had once said—'All roads lead to Amber'—and I wondered then, as I do now, at the difference the choice may make, despite the end's apparent inevitability to those of your blood."

"You know?" I said. "You understand?"

"I think so."

He nodded, then pointed.

"That is the real Amber down there, isn't it?"

"Yes," I said. "Yes, it is."